Save

Our

SOULS

Volume 2

Jeff Mixon

Save Our Souls Volume 2 © 2015 by Jeff Mixon.

For information contact:
info@uptownmediaventures.com

Book and Cover design by Team Uptown

ISBN: 978-1-68121-018-6

First Edition: April 2015

"Whatever we cherish that tends to lessen our love for God or to interfere

with the service *due* Him, of *that* do we make a god."

Ellen G. White, *Patriarchs and Prophets*

Page left blank intentionally

Dedication

This book is dedicated to my immediate family members, living and deceased: Hughery Mixon (father), Georgia Mixon (mother), Larry Buchanan, Gregory Buchanan, Sharon Rose, Victor Mixon, Charles Mixon and Captain Rico Mixon. Thank you for your unconditional love and support throughout the years! *I love you all!*

Thank you, Father!

Thank you, Son!

Thank you, Holy Spirit!

Page left blank intentionally

Chapter   Page

Page left blank intentionally

The Divine Law

"**A**n expert in religious law tried to trap Him with this question: 'Teacher, which is the most important commandment in the laws of Moses?'"

"Jesus replied, 'You must love the Lord your God with all your heart, all your soul and all your mind. This is the first and greatest commandment. A second is equally important: Love your neighbor as yourself. The entire law and all the demands of the prophets are based on these two commandments.'"

The *Divine Law* encompasses the *Ten Commandments* with a particular emphasis on the first commandment: "Thou shall have no other god before me."

Fresh out of Egypt, the Israelites made a habit of blatant idol worship. The application of the first commandment to daily behavior in modern times is a bit more complicated. In *Patriarchs and Prophets*, however, the Prophetess Ellen White clarifies the first commandment with a captivating brand of prose: "Whatever we cherish," she writes, "that tends to lessen our love for God or to interfere with the service *due* Him, of *that* do we make a god."

Glory. Supremacy. Admiration. Respect. Approval. Power. Wealth. Cars. Houses. Jewelry. Sex. Television. Sports. *Even vengeance.*

Whichever of these we cherish more than we cherish serving our Creator we have turned into *our god;* placing that god — who can never quench our spiritual thirst -- above the God that provides the very food that we eat and the very water that we drink.

Obedience to the first commandment is a shield against thoughts and reactions capable of creating disharmony within our most cherished possession — our souls.

Prologue

How would you react if you began having dreams about people you've never met - if those dreams began to come true? What if the dreams began stretching further and further into the future, playing out always with eerie precision? For most people, these questions are impossible to answer. Experiencing one paradigm shift in a lifetime is extraordinary. For those endowed with the ability to discern its spiritual relevance, the election of 2008 represented a paradigm shift. But, what seemed like a big deal at the time was a mere precursor of things to come. Occurring without clear recognition of God's controlling hand, the ensuing rancor of the *Tea Party* masked the unity and love that the election inspired in the most powerful country on earth. Nevertheless, it *shook* the leaders of the global political and economic structure the Bible refers to as *Babylon*.

The *Tribulation Period*, a seven year period of supernatural turmoil, will end with our Lord and Savior Jesus Christ returning on a cloud (Daniel 7:13-14 & Revelation 14:14). This book outlines a series of future world events occurring in the years just prior to the

Tribulation Period - a time of enormous hope and massive confusion.

> "In the last days I will pour out my Spirit upon all people. Your sons and daughters will prophesy. Your young men will see visions, and old men will dream dreams."

Acts 2:17

Save Our Souls is the tale of an ordinary group of people from Akron and Cleveland, Ohio. Declared "unnatural threats to the safety and security of the United States of America" in the year 2021, they are forced into hiding by the *Department of Homeland Security*. They don't know how many of them there are or *why* they were chosen to receive an outpouring of God's Spirit. At the climax of the cosmic struggle for redemption, however, they find themselves on the front line of a battle against Satan's minions. Fortunately, they have the aid of a *powerful, faithful companion*.

Chapter 1

The Book Of Acts

"In those days I will pour out my Spirit even on my servants – men and women alike – and they will prophesy."

ACTS 2:18

Pastor Ricky must have left Chicago within minutes of receiving the shocking news of Lyla speaking with a German accent. Seven hours later, the concerned pastor bursts through the hospital doors like a movie character. Lyla's mother, Champagne and Brian are the only family members still present at the hospital when he arrives. After purchasing ginger ales for everybody from the first floor vending machine, Brian catches up with Pastor Ricky just as he is entering Lyla's room. They're relieved to see him, especially after the most recent turn of events. Not one of them says a word, though, as he observes Lyla speaking with the German accent.

Running to hug her big brother, Champagne squeezes him hard. Pastor Ricky is unable to move with her body draped over him. Eyes closed, it looks as though Champagne is praying.

Pastor Ricky waits for a minute, attempting to console her.

"It'll be okay, sweetheart."

Lyla's mother, though, is getting impatient.

"Champagne, come drink some soda," she says.

Approaching the bed slowly, Lyla's brother listens then looks at his mother.

"I think she's speaking in tongues."

This was another unexpected twist to the saga. As strange as it sounded, Brian thought, it gave them hope that the situation might end on a positive note. At least it implied that there was nothing wrong with Lyla medically. And, if there was ever two candidates to speak in tongues, Lyla and her big brother had his votes. They were the most committed Christians that he had ever met. What this might mean for their relationship was a whole different matter. Brian never saw Lyla and him being equally yoked spiritually. He was barely a babe in Christ. For now, the only thing that mattered, however, was Lyla awakening without serious medical problems.

"Speaking in tongue?" Mrs. Johnson echoed. "Are you sure?"

Pastor Ricky hesitates, raising doubt in Brian's mind.

"I know an easy way to find out," he says, reaching in his pocket for his phone.

Pressing a few buttons, he holds it next to Lyla's mouth; recording her. When Lyla takes an extended break from speaking, he presses more buttons.

"I'll send this recording to Father Lawson. We should hear something in a couple of hours."

"Who is Bishop Matthias?"

"We don't know," his mother responds. "She's mentioned his name a few times."

Less than thirty minutes later, Pastor Ricky receives a phone call from Father Lawson.

"Really? A nighttime rainbow. That's interesting. I wouldn't miss seeing one of those for the world."

Pastor Ricky laughs then, realizing that his mother and Brian have no clue what's going on, he begins speaking for their benefit.

"My little sister is definitely speaking in tongues. She's predicted this strange rainbow? And she definitely doesn't trust Bishop Matthias? Thank you, Father Lawson. I need to take care of some business. When do you think you'll have time to review the recording more completely?"

He laughs again. Father Lawson must have a pretty good sense of humor, Brian thinks to himself.

"Great! Why don't you give me a call tomorrow evening around seven? Great! And thanks again."

He laughs.

"I'll be looking forward to it."

"Well," he says, hanging up the phone. "He thinks Lyla will be okay. That's the most important thing. And as you heard, she does appear to be speaking in tongues, maybe even prophesying."

Listening to Pastor Ricky explain the details to his mother, Brian becomes overwhelmed by the talk of rainbows, prophesying and speaking in tongues. Lyla still hasn't awakened, yet. Watching her lie there helplessly, all he can think of is preparing a nice meal for her. She hasn't eaten anything in days. He convinces himself that she might awaken at any moment. This is what he wants to believe. When she awakens, he plans to hold her in his arms, kiss her beautiful face and serve her two favorite meals to her in bed. Lyla could never decide whether she liked Chicken Alfredo or Chicken Quesadillas with jalapeño peppers best. It was one of their running jokes. Brian decides to cook both of them. Just in case, he'll also stock up on the wine.

Brian feels as though he's about to faint himself.

Pastor Ricky and his mother are rightfully proud about Lyla speaking in tongues. Brian's proud, too. Yet, he finds it difficult to share their sudden and tremendous faith. Choosing to rest his mind on a thought that will keep him grounded, he focuses on preparing a meal for Lyla's return home.

Not wanting to be alone, he calls Carlos up and invites him to go shopping with him. His schedule was tied up for the rest of the day. So, they made plans to go the next evening.

When visiting hours end, Mrs. Johnson presses her face against Lyla's gently.

"Rest up, my beautiful angel. God has something exciting in store for you."

Each day at the hospital Brian had been tempted to ask Lyla's mother for time alone with Lyla. But, a sense of guilt made everything feel so awkward.

The following night, he left his jacket in Lyla's room on purpose so that he would have an excuse to go back to her room alone. When he returned to the third floor, however, the jacket was already at the receptionist desk. A beautiful, middle-age Arab woman handed it to him, asking if he was related to Lyla.

"She's my girlfriend," he told her. "I haven't had a moment alone with her."

She looked around quickly.

"I think she's alone right now. Maybe I'll put this nice jacket back where I found it."

She winks at Brian, bringing a huge smile to his face.

"Follow me."

"Thank you, miss!"

"Don't take too long."

As the receptionist walks away, he pauses for a few seconds. A lot has happened since he last spoke with Lyla. A week ago, Celeste was a mere nuisance, not a drug dealer. Lyla wasn't suspected of having supernatural gifts. He hadn't betrayed her trust, and she wasn't in the hospital in a coma. All that had changed now. There were rainbows and prophesying and speaking in tongues. None of those things, extraordinary as they were, mattered now; not while this beautiful, young angel lied in a hospital bed – unable to reconnect with the world.

He wasn't sure what to say to Lyla. Dropping to his knees at the side of her bed, he begins to pray; convinced that this is what Lyla would do if it were him lying in that bed. In Jesus' name, he prays for her to wake up; safe and healthy. He prays that they'll get past these extraordinary events; enjoying a happy life together. He confesses his sins to God, particularly where Celeste is concerned. In dealing with Celeste, he betrayed Lyla and everything that she stood for. Even if it meant dealing with drama, here and there, Lyla maintained a personal code of ethical behavior consistent with her faith. With this in mind, he promised God that he would do things the right way from here on out.

Finally, he prayed for God to protect Lyla from any harm that might result from involving her in his plan for human salvation. Lyla was, for the most part, a simple, easy-going woman. But, if God saw fit to include her in one of His divine projects, he didn't see how He could have made a better choice. Figuratively speaking, Lyla possessed an inner beauty that could move mountains.

When he finishes praying, he takes a long look at Lyla. Hugging her, he kisses her on the lips before leaving.

He left the jacket again, by mistake this time.

Carlos calls just as Brian is starting his car.

"How you doin' bro?"

Brian lies. It's the only way to keep from breaking down. He can only hope that God will understand.

"Not bad. The doctors expect Lyla to wake up at any moment."

It's the first lie that he remembers telling to convince himself, not someone else, that things would be okay. Or, maybe it was a genuine display of faith.

"We headed to the grocery store first?"

"Yeah, I'm making Lyla's favorite meal."

"Which one?" he asks, amused.

He'd, obviously, had a few drinks.

"Both of them."

"That a boy! Lyla's a good woman. It must be tough on you."

He didn't know the half of it.

"I'm trying to keep positive thoughts. I wanna be ready when she wakes up. Is Jerry around?"

"No."

"Why?"

"I was just wondering."

A half hour later, Carlos and Brian walk through the grocery store. Skipping the entire conversation regarding rainbows and speaking in tongues, he jumps straight to the arrest.

"Did you get my message the other day?"

"Sure did. I don't know what to tell you, bro. Kayla was here the day that Jerry was running his mouth. He'd been drinking, of course."

"It's cool."

"I didn't even know that Kayla knew Celeste," he adds.

This is bad news. Brian doesn't want to look suspicious by asking the questions on his mind, but he had to know.

"Did my name come up?"

"Let me see."

A pause.

"I don't remember your name being mentioned. Why?"

"No reason. I just have to be careful what I say around Jerry. I keep forgetting that he's a police officer. I thought I might have said something that I shouldn't have."

"About Celeste?"

"Yeah, we think that's why Lyla fainted."

An awkward pause.

Brian had leaked the information of Celeste's "after-church" activities to Jerry in a manner designed to conceal his intent. But, even drunk, he might have seen through this ploy. Everyone was on pins and needles, and Lyla was in the hospital. How did he fuck things up so bad?

"Earth to Brian."

"Huh?"

"You sure you're okay, bro?"

"Yeah, I'm good. I just have a lot on my mind."

"No shit! I thought I came shopping with you, but you're the one with an empty shopping cart."

Looking down, Brian shakes his head.

"My fault, dude. Where's my shopping list?"

He pats both front pockets, first; then the back ones.

"Here it is. Let's see, I need cheese."

Carlos' sense of humor turns out to be the perfect antidote to the heavy thoughts burdening his soul. After purchasing everything he needed for Lyla's meal, he orders a pizza to help wash down the case of beer that Carlos bought. They top off their personal shopping with two jars of salsa and huge bags of potato and salsa chips. Brian looks forward to an ice cold beer. It'll be the first drop of alcohol to enter his system since the news on Sunday that Lyla had been rushed to the hospital.

It's Friday night. The date is June 17, 2021.

That night, Carlos and Brian walked into the grocery store as two regular guys with a couple of hours to kill. They exited the store as witnesses to the most amazing sight that their eyes had ever seen; a futuristic, celestial amusement park. Looking upwards in awe, Brian thought he had to be dreaming. A fluorescent rainbow stood out against the darkened sky, a rainbow reaching as far as the eye could see.

"Hello," he says, answering my phone, all but speechless.

It's Champagne.

"Brian," she says, bursting with excitement. "I'm playing in the rainbow. Beam me up, God!"

On some level, he can appreciate the excited reaction of a child to something so sublime. At the same time, he's overwhelmed by the beauty and craziness of this futuristic occurrence.

"That's sounds fun, Champagne. Let me call you back."

Looking back, even as an adult, he might have reacted in a similar manner to Champagne on this warm summer night had he not felt horrified by this fact: his girlfriend predicted this rainbow while lying in a hospital bed - in a coma.

Pastor Ricky called next.

"Hello."

"Brian?"

"Sure is. How's it going Pastor Ricky?"

"You outside?"

"Yep."

"What do you think?"

"Well, this definitely a rainbow. My entire body is showered in fluorescent, green light. I see some orange people. I see some red people. Some people are cheering; others are down on their knees praying."

"Yeah. It's hard to know what to make of it. If Lyla didn't seem so adamant that there was something crooked about Bishop Matthias, I'd be down on my knees worshipping with the people around me."

Brian's other line rings again.

"Can you hold for a minute, Pastor Ricky?"

Seeing that the call is from the hospital, Brian becomes alarmed.

"Hey, baby! I'm hungry!"

"Lyla?"

"It's me, baby. The doctor told me what happened. I hope I didn't scare everybody."

"Oh, my God. I can't believe it. I was so worried about you. Oh, my goodness. I don't even know where to start. Can you come home, yet?"

"Not yet. The doctors want to run some tests tomorrow."

"How do you feel?"

"I feel great. I'm just hungry."

"Hell, I don't blame you. You haven't eaten in a week. You don't know how happy I am to hear your voice."

"Dude, I'm so happy for you," Carlos says, still a little freaked out by the rainbow. "Tell Lyla that I hope she feels better."

"Carlos says 'hello'."

"Tell Carlos that I said 'hi'."

"She said 'hello.' Man, I wish I could come see you right now."

"Me, too. I'm so hungry."

"Hold on a minute," he says, getting an idea. "I have your brother on the other line."

He clicks over.

"Let me call you back, pastor. It's Lyla. She's awake."

"Well, hallelujah! Please Brian. Call me right back."

"Okay."

"Tell Lyla that I said 'hello'."

"Okay, I'll call you right back."

"Brian!"

"Yes."

"Lyla may not remember everything. I wouldn't say too much to her beyond the fact that she fainted."

"Gotcha!"

"Don't even mention the arrest if she doesn't bring it up first."

Anxious to get back to Lyla, he takes a deep breath. Pausing for a moment, he assures Pastor Ricky that it's safe to allow him to speak to his girlfriend.

"The only thing that I'm gong to mention is that she fainted. No Celeste, no tongues and definitely no rainbow predictions. I wonder if she's looked out of the window, yet."

"Hopefully not."

Brian pauses, contemplating what it might mean if Lyla remembers everything.

"I'd better go."

Click.

"Hey, Lyla. I'm sorry. That was your brother. He told me to tell you 'hello.' Are you sure you feel okay? You were out for a week."

"I feel pretty good."

"Do you know why you're in the hospital?"

"The nurse told me that I fainted."

Brian hears voices in the background.

"Excuse me, Brian."

"Sure."

He can make out a conversation but can't make out the words.

"Brian, the doctor's here. I'm going to have to call you back in the morning."

"That's okay, baby. Get some rest. I'm glad to hear that you're feeling better."

"I love you, baby."

"I love you, too. Always! I'll be sure to let your family know that you're feeling better. Okay?"

"Okay."

"I'll see you in the morning."

"Wow," Carlos says, giving Brian a high-five, "I know that's a huge relief."

"Wow is right!" Brian said with a huge smile. "My baby's awake!"

"Just in time to see the rainbow."

"Oh yeah," he sighs, "the rainbow."

Since the nurse had to tell Lyla that she had fainted, it was a safe bet that she didn't remember much. Hopefully, she'd just relax; not have to deal with any undue stress.

The next day, the hospital was a zoo. According to a receptionist, there were at least thirty visitors – and phone calls. Shortly after 3:00 p.m., Lyla was finally released. The zoo then moved to her mother's house. Not until after 8:00 p.m. - when she, Pastor Ricky and Brian left for her house - did she receive a moment's peace.

Chapter 2

The Book Of Daniel

"Relax, Pastor Ricky. You don't have to worry about me freaking out. I just wanna make sure I have the facts straight. Maybe I'm trippin' or something."

"Trust me, Brian," he interrupts. "You have the facts straight."

"So, not only did we have this crazy-looking nighttime rainbow for the first time ever; a Catholic Bishop, this Bishop Matthias or Father Matthias – or whoever the fuck he is - predicted it a week ahead of time. And Lyla predicted both his prediction and that crazy-ass rainbow."

"Yes."

"Well, that's a relief. AT LEAST THERE'S NOTHING CRAZY GOING ON AROUND THIS MOTHAFUCKA!"

Lyla looks as if she wants to slap Brian.

Pastor Ricky cocks his head to one side suddenly, as if entertaining some new thought.

"Do we know for sure," he asks, "that there's never been a nighttime rainbow?"

Underwhelmed by the implication, Brian overreacts - again.

"*THERE'S NEVER BEEN ONE OF THOSE!*" he answers, unaware of just how rude he sounds. "*That wasn't a regular rainbow. It was bright and fluorescent. It was RIGHT NEXT TO US. People WALKED in it — turned yellow and orange and green and red. That was NOT A REGULAR FUCKIN' RAINBOW!*"

Annoyed, Lyla rolls her eyes.

"Why are you rolling your eyes at me? he asks, defending myself. "I didn't grow up holier than thou."

She walks away.

"What?"

When Lyla returns, she hands Brian a glass of wine.

"Drink this."

"*Thanks, Nurse Johnson.*"

Holding onto the glass, he hasn't decided whether or not he is in the mood for drinking. This is a first.

Lyla turns to her brother.

"Would you like something cold to drink?"

"You can bring me another glass of this wine," Brian interrupts, before drinking it in a single gulp.

Grabbing the glass, Lyla rolls her eyes again.

"I cooked your favorite meal," he shouts as she exits the room.

"Which one?" she shouts back, sarcastically.

"Both of them: Chicken Alfredo and Chicken Quesadillas with jalapeño peppers."

Brian realized that he was being a bit of an asshole, but the rainbow and the prediction had him more freaked out than he realized. The entire week had been a strain on his psyche. It's only a matter of time, he knew, before someone mentioned Celeste.

"I guess I should say 'thanks,'" Lyla shouts.

He can't help smiling at this one.

"It would be nice, smarty-pants!"

No matter how crazy things seem, the one thing that isn't in doubt is that he's thrilled to see Lyla back to her old perky self.

"I made plenty, pastor. You're always welcomed to eat with us."

"No thanks. I'm having dinner at Grandma Georgia's."

Lyla returns with two tall glasses of orange juice. She hands one to her brother, setting the other down on a coaster.

"What about me?"

Without answering, she walks back into the kitchen, returning quicker this time. In one hand, she holds a full glass of wine; in the other, an unopened bottle of wine.

"Here."

"Thank you."

"You might wanna drink this one a little slower."

"Maybe you should bring Jesus a glass. He's liable to walk through the door at any moment."

It's obvious that Pastor Ricky is annoyed by the statement. He looks at Lyla. Lyla is annoyed, too, but manages to maintain her composure. Not sure how to respond, Brian takes a sip of wine.

"Sorry yall. It must be the wine."

Judging by the intense silence, no one is buying this. He prays that they can just get past it, but he's at a loss for words to change the topic. It's too late. In her gentle way, Lyla begins digging in.

"Is that what you're afraid of?"

This catches Brian off guard.

"Who says I'm afraid?"

"You don't have to be afraid."

Suddenly, he's uncomfortable. Lyla sees something in him that he hasn't even seen yet. Having successfully done so, though, he thinks it's time for her to back off a little.

"Lyla," he says, upset with her now, "I think I'll be okay."

Lyla presses the issue.

"Nothing bad is going to happen when Jesus returns."

She looks at her brother for confirmation. He offers little more than a curious stare. He's probably thinking the same thing that Brian's thinking. According to the *Book of Revelation*, a whole lot of bad things happen when Jesus returns.

As usual, though, Lyla is thinking more logically.

"Since the *Tribulation Period* hasn't started, yet," she says, "*our loving Lord and Savior* (she punches me in the arm) won't be arriving today, tomorrow or any time in the next seven years. And the Bible didn't say anything

Jeff Mixon

about the people receiving an outpouring of God's spirit being harmed."

Based on Pastor Ricky's teachings and the *Book of Daniel*, Brian agreed with the first point. But, what was this stuff about "people receiving an outpouring of God's spirit"?

"Say that second part again," he requests, confused.

"Acts 2:17," Pastor Ricky says, introspectively. "'In the last days, I will pour out my Spirit upon all people. Your sons and daughters will prophesy. Your young men will see visions, and your old men will dream dreams.'"

Lyla, just realizing what she has said, pauses. They had been operating according to different world paradigms. For the very first time, their quiet conversation had given Brian a small glimpse of an eternal truth. He couldn't remember the words exactly, but he understood the meaning: "Revelations; upon this rock I will build my church, and all the powers of hell will not conquer it."

Although he didn't see the full truth right away, his eyes began to open to the possibility of a new, earth-shaking reality.

"I don't think we have anything to fear from God," Pastor Ricky continues. "Trouble may be brewing on the earth. If Lyla is called to act, however, I'm confident that she'll be working under the protection of a powerful, faithful companion."

"Look," he said, pointing to the television "Let me turn up the volume."

Bishop Matthias was holding a press conference.

"He's lying," Lyla says emphatically, without even taking time to listen to what he was saying.

Judging from the look on her face, it's obvious that she dislikes this man that she has never met before intensely. It seems a little strange, but *strange* had suddenly become the norm.

'This is crazy,' Brian thinks, looking at his name plastered across the screen.

"So this is it?"

"It appears so," Pastor Ricky says with an ominous stare.

Looking down at his watch now, something seems wrong.

"What wrong?' Lyla asks.

"I'll call you this afternoon," he says, gathering his things together quickly.

"What is it?" Lyla asks.

"I need to get going. Celeste and I have a 7 a.m. prayer session."

Having lost the "I'm-new-to-spiritual-matters" argument hands down, this was one of the few times that Brian didn't look forward to being alone with Lyla. But she had other ideas. Pastor Ricky is barely out the door before he feels her pressing against him from behind, wrapping her arms around his waist.

"Hey sexy," she says. "You got a minute?"

"Sure, anything for you."

"Maybe you can help me out."

Brian's mind is still partially scrambled from anxiety. He feels her hard nipples press against his back. After a week without physical contact, it's amazing that he doesn't feel like jumping her right away. Under the circumstances, he's a little surprised that she's has no qualms about engaging in a sinful act. When it came to spiritual matters, however, it was becoming obviously that he simply didn't get it.

As always, though, Lyla was on top of things. Instead of appealing to his animal instincts the way she normally would, she chose instead to introduce him to the art of spiritual seduction.

"When I tried to keep the law," she whispers, nibbling his left ear, "it condemned me."

Having never heard scripture recited in such a sexy, seductive manner, he finds himself captivated.

"So, I died to the law," she continues, unbuttoning his shirt from behind. "I stopped trying to meet all its requirements..."

Pausing, Lyla turns him around slowly.

"... so that I might live for God."

He wasn't sure what all of this meant, but it sounded good to him. Excited to discover that scripture could sound so sexy, he was more than happy to yield to Lyla's authority on religious matters.

"What was that?" he asks, as Lyla's presses her soft cheek against his well-developed chest muscles.

"Shut up and take your pants off."

Still just a little apprehensive, he asks: "Are you sure you're up for this?"

Jeff Mixon

"I *predict* that it will help."

"*Predict*," he mutters, "at least one of them still has a sense of humor."

Chapter 3

Eyes On God

Lying in bed, Brian rolls over on his back to look at Lyla. They've already eaten breakfast. Lyla has just returned from a morning bath. He can't remember what he asked her, but he remembers her response. It was pretty intense. Walking over from the mirror, she sits on the bed then rolls on top of him. His pleasure center is inundated with soft skin and expensive perfume. Staring at him intensely with those beautiful, light-brown eyes, she kisses him deeply.

"I think we should talk."

"Whatever, you're up to," he smiles, "you have my full cooperation."

"Shut up," she laughs, "I'm trying to be serious."

He has to get out another laugh before achieving serious mode.

"You still have my cooperation. Can I have one more kiss, though?"

They smooch.

"Thank you."

"You're welcome. Can I start now?"

"Yes, you may."

"Brian," her confession begins, "before I awakened, I heard Jesus' voice."

Whoa! He wasn't expecting this. Two dreams and a prediction; something was definitely going on.

"In a dream," Lyla continues, "I was wearing the suit jacket that I found in my room when I woke up. Jesus tells me to go to my king; then, when I wake up, I see the jacket from the dream. *Your* jacket!"

Brian was touched deeply by this but couldn't come up with anything to say right away. Finally, he confesses his prayer.

"I prayed for you, Lyla," he admits. "I was worried about you. I knelt down next to you and prayed that god would protect you. When I was talking to God, for the first time, I spoke like I was speaking to another person. I have a relationship with God, Lyla – thanks to you."

Lyla's confession allayed his fears that the outpouring of God's spirit upon her would lead to their separation. He imagined that Lyla would become famous like Bishop Matthias, maybe end up on the news or the *Kerry*

Washington Show. He imagined a life of fame and fortune for her. That, however, changed over night. The very next day, the *Department of Homeland Security* arrested a Hispanic man who accurately predicted a Palestinian uprising; declaring him an "unnatural threat to the safety and security of the United States of America." The news of a sudden round up spread like wildfire.

Pastor Ricky alerted everyone that knew about Lyla prophesying that they needed to start denying that it had occurred. To Lyla, he warned: "Don't get too caught up in all the hoopla. Keep your eyes on God."

Chapter 4

Trouble Brewing

Looking over some of Pastor Ricky's old e-mails, Brian was more intrigued by his understanding of politics than the spiritual stuff. His description of the *Pre-Tribulation Period* sounded a lot like the present. Corporations and their front groups began to militarize as the citizens unified.

The end of the *Tribulation Period*, he pointed out, would be marked by the return of Jesus Christ; as described in the books of *Daniel* and *Revelation*.

Fueled by Bishop Matthias' inflammatory rhetoric, news of the round-up of so-called "unnatural threats to the safety and security of the United States of America" took the country by storm. The bishop never explained how those being rounded up presented a threat to national security. But, repeated references to Matthew 24: 24 provided the *Department of Homeland Security* a pretext for action.

During the news conference, Lyla kept referring to Bishop Matthias as Antiochus.

"Who is Antiochus?" Brian finally asked.

Pastor Ricky responds by slapping a Bible against his chest. When he opens it, Lyla decides to put in her two cents.

"Brian has his own Bible. Why don't you go and get it?"

"Yes," the pastor agrees. "Perfect time for a Bible study."

"It is?"

Smiling, Lyla gives him the gotcha look.

"Yeah, let's have Bible study."

"Whoa! Wait a minute. What just happened here?"

He doesn't feel at all amused.

"Bible study? Right now?"

When Lyla sticks her tongue out, Brian feels like slapping it. Surprisingly, Pastor Ricky, steps in to chastise her. He feels better, and a little surprised, by Lyla's obedient reaction. As she quietly leaves the room to get her Bible, Pastor Ricky notices the astonished look on Brian's face.

"We have a little agreement about Bible study," he smiles. "And yes! It *is* fun."

Smiling broadly, Brian decides to rub it in a little.

"That's right!" he says, loud enough for Lyla to hear him.

Before he realizes that she has made her way back into the room, Brian makes a clumsy reference to her speaking in tongues: *"I wouldn't care if she started speaking in Spanish."*

Neither Lyla nor her brother finds this funny. Outvoted 2 to 1, he decides that it's time to get serious.

"I'll go get my Bible."

Antiochus Epiphanes, the ruler of Syria from 175-163 B.C., turns out to be one of many antichrists. Yet, he was more significant that the others. Attacking the Jewish homeland, Antiochus puts a stop to their religious teachings. This is one of actions foreshadowing *the Anti-Christ* of *Revelation*.

The media must have shown the clip of Bishop Matthias' dramatic recitation of Matthew 24: 24 a hundred times per day:

"For false messiahs....."

He hesitates.

"And false prophets....."

An even more dramatic pause.

"Will rise up and perform GREAT SIGNS and WONDERS....."

Looking towards the sky as if he expected Jesus to return, then and there, Bishop Mathias holds both hands upward. Adjusting his gaze, he speaks to the camera with great sincerity.

"So as to DECEIVE, if possible, even GOD'S CHOSEN PEOPLE."

"Boy, he's good!" exclaims Pastor Ricky.

"He's the false prophet," Lyla says, scornfully.

Brian turns to look at her.

"Are you saying that the rainbow was a faked miracle?"

"No. I'm saying that Bishop Matthias didn't predict it. Whoever did is probably locked up - or dead."

Brian turns to Pastor Ricky.

Neither of Pastor Ricky nor Brian doubts her words. With a round-up and a potential murder, though, there seems to be no limit as to how serious things might get.

"Pastor Ricky," he asks, noticeably concerned. "What is Lyla's role in all of this?"

He doesn't answer right away, allowing Brian time to amend the question.

"Should we assume that she has a role?"

Once again, Pastor Ricky is slow to answer. But this time, Brian waits.

"It certainly appears so," he says, finally.

Based on the expression on Lyla's face, it's obvious that she is annoyed by the question.

"Stop worrying about me, Brian," she complains, before walking away.

Shaking his head, Brian looks at the pastor. The commitment in Lyla's eyes, voice and body language is fearless.

This, more than anything, scares him.

Chapter 5

Dreaming Dreams

A world that seemed so mundane until Brian met Lyla continued to change at a rapid pace.

The first time one of his dreams materialized and he was dumbfounded. Had it not been for Sharon, a girl that he had never met before, he might have chalked it up to a case of déjà vu. Everything that Sharon did or said, though, matched the meaningless dream that occurred two nights earlier. Normally, he didn't remember his dreams, but this one had a vivid, peculiar quality.

His reaction, upon meeting Sharon, was very awkward. Based on Lyla's scornful look, she picked up the unusual vibe right away. Sharon was dark, beautiful, and exotic-looking. Lyla had likely misinterpreted his awkward reaction as a sign of attraction. She wasn't too concerned to leave us alone, however, when Sharon mentioned that she was thirsty.

"Is there a problem?" she asks when Lyla is safely inside the house.

Brian was thrown off more by Sharon's boldness. Embarrassed; he played it off as best he could.

"No," he said, shaking his head to reassure her. "I'm… I'm sorry. I didn't sleep too well last night."

Rubbing his eyes as if it might somehow increase the flow of oxygen to his brain, the situation was starting to freak Brian out. As she did in the dream, Lyla returns with three bottles of bottled of water. Handing the first one to Sharon, she hands Brian the second one. He opens it for her. Then, they switched bottles.

"Let's go inside," Lyla says to Sharon after watching her take two huge, satisfying gulps of the ice cold liquid.

When Sharon is inside, she flashes a disdainful look in Brian's direction. Stopping just inside the door, he decides that this would be a good time for a walk. He needs to get away from Lyla and Sharon. A good walk might help him regain his composure.

"You two go ahead. I'm gonna run to the store. Anybody need anything?"

That strange feeling hits him again when he realizes that he spoke these exact same words in the dream. He convinces himself that this is all a coincidence. He must have seen Sharon at a family function a while back without really noticing her. Lyla's mother quickly disabuses him of this notion when she asks him to play the lottery for her. Panic really begins to set in now. 'If Mrs. Johnson asks me to play 908 straight for two dollars,' he tells himself, 'this is more than a series of coincidences.'

"Put two dollars on 908 for me – straight."

She says this while searching through her purse for change. Either he's dreaming right now, or something other-worldly is going on. It was one thing to witness Lyla speaking in tongues. In the black church, it's not unusual to witness people speaking in tongue. Brian always believed that they were faking, though. Pastor Ricky described speaking in tongue in a way that perfectly matched what Lyla had done. She spoke in an "unfamiliar but *known* language." The people claiming to speak in tongue were merely babbling. At least there is general agreement in the church community that speaking in tongue was a biblical phenomenon that continues to occur. He never known anyone to claim that their dreams materialized exactly the way they dreamed them. Unlike Lyla, he was still a "Babe in Christ."

Jeff Mixon

"Don't worry about it, Mrs. Johnson. I have a couple of extra dollars. You can pay me back when you win."

She wouldn't win, of course. If his dream was correct, 209 would fall instead. Afraid that Lyla, Sharon and Ms. Johnson might think he was losing it, he didn't dare mention this to them. He would find out soon enough just how different things had become.

He played 908 straight for two dollars and played 209 ten times. Returning from the store he gave Lyla's mother her ticket and one of the tickets that he purchased. He couldn't resist. Lyla's mother was always playing the lottery. She rarely won. Yet, the mere possibility of winning temporarily improved her mood.

"209?" she says, examining the tickets closely. "Are both of these for me?"

"Yep."

"When did you start playing numbers?"

"I don't. I kept seeing the number 209 yesterday and decided to give it a try."

He held one of the tickets in his hand. The rest were stored inside his wallet.

"Thank you!"

"You're welcome."

"Maybe you'll have beginners luck."

Entering the living room, Brian notices that Sharon is wearing the same pearl earrings that she wore in the dream. He then recognizes her entire outfit.

"I'm headed up for a nap, Lyla."

He felt a little sick to the stomach.

"It was nice meeting you Sharon."

When he closed his eyes it was 4:47 p.m. A couple of hours later he awakened, feeling refreshed, yet apprehensive. It was 7:14 p.m. For a few moments, he considers the possibility that he had dreamed the earlier part of the day. No such luck. Reaching into his back pocket, he produces the lottery tickets.

Hurrying down the attic stairs to the bathroom, he rinses his face and brushes his teeth. He returns to the attic at 7:29 p.m. - six minutes before the winning lottery number will be revealed.

At 7:34 p.m., he decides that he doesn't want to be alone in the attic, anymore. He quickly head down the steps to grab a beer from the refrigerator. Before he can make it to the first floor, he hears Lyla's mother scream.

"Brian! Brian!" Lyla yells.

He almost runs her over entering the kitchen.

"Your number won!"

Pretending to be surprised, he hugs her. Lifting her into the air, he presses his face against her buxom. Almost afraid to open his eyes, he wishes that he could hold her in his arms for the rest of the day. Subconsciously, he knows what has just happened. He senses the enormous responsibility that Lyla and he will have to live up to.

Brian continues pretending to be shocked and exuberant for everyone else's sake. But, when Sharon leaves, he eases his way back up to the attic. he needed to be alone. Lying on the bed on his back he closes his eyes. Clearing his mind completely, he falls asleep for almost an hour. He awakens to the sound of Lyla's voice and the sensation of her soft hand beneath his shirt. He realizes that she is lying in the bed next to him.

"What's wrong, baby?" she asks, aware now that something is bothering him.

"We need to talk, Lyla," he says, reaching into his back pocket for the rest of the tickets. "Look at these."

Examining the tickets, her mouth drops open.

"Are all of these winning tickets?"

"Mmm. Hmm."

Opening her mouth to speak again, she quickly covers it with her hand to keep from blurting her thoughts out. She knows exactly what is happening but seeks confirmation.

Whispering, she asks: "Did you *know* that this was the winning number?"

"Mmm. Hmm."

"How?"

Still struggling to come to grips with what's happening, Brian explains as best he can.

"I dreamed everything that happened today two nights ago. Your friend Sharon was in the dream, and I've never seen her before today."

"Wow! I'm excited for you!"

"Because of the money?"

"No. We have to give the money to charity."

"We do?"

"Yes, we do."

"Does it say that in the Bible?"

Jeff Mixon

Without skipping a beat, Lyla recites Matthew 19: 21, "'If you want to be perfect, go and sell all your possessions and give the money to the poor, and you will have treasure in Heaven. Then come, follow me.'"

He didn't see how she interpreted that to mean they had to give the money back, but he knew that there was no way he would win the argument.

"I'm proud of you," Lyla continues, smiling brightly.

"Thank you."

He was still confused about why he had to give the money to charity. Maybe God wanted him to put a down payment on an engagement ring.

Lyla and Brian eventually return to the kitchen, holding hands.

"Thank you, Brian," Mrs. Johnson says, hugging him. "I don't know who taught you how to pick numbers. But be sure to let me know the next time you get a hot one."

"I will."

It felt good for Brian to see Mrs. Johnson smile, especially at him.

"Congratulations, mom," Lyla says, kissing her on the cheek. "Brian and I have to get back to the house."

This was one of the first times that Brian remembered Ms. Johnson taking the time to walk them to the door. She never tried to come between them, but she never embraced Brian with open arms. Like most African-American mothers, she simply watched with a skeptical eye. Walking out the door, though, he feels as if they've finally put the incident at Champagne's school behind them.

Lyla is in a super mood on the ride to her house. It doesn't seem to matter to her as much as it should that he needs both hands to drive. Every time that she speaks, she grabs and holds his right hand.

"Baby, God *spoke* to you."

He thought about this for a second. Lyla always said that if God hands you a rake, He doesn't want you to stand around holding it. He wants you to rake the leaves. If this was indeed a spiritual gift on the par with Lyla's, what leaves did God want him to rake? How exactly does it work, he wondered? He had a dream two nights earlier but none the previous night. There was no guarantee that he'd ever have another prophetic dream. He was grateful for the one. But, unlike Lyla's situation, the dream didn't point him in any particular direction.

Lyla's determination to give the money to charity didn't dampen his plan to buy her an engagement ring.

"I'm glad you took a nap earlier," she smiles, still holding my right hand. "After we eat and have a glass of wine - after I finish making love to you - I want to go dancing."

A glass of wine sounded good. A case sounded even better. Maybe it would make him forget about the dream for a while. It was the leaf-raking that bothered him. He wasn't sure that he was up to the task.

They finally made it home.

"You nervous?" Lyla asks, exiting the car on his side, still holding his hand.

"Yeah, I'm a little nervous."

Turning Brian towards her, she catches his face in the soft palms of her hands.

"Remember, baby, 'God don't pick the qualified. He qualifies the picked.' If he has something in store for you, it won't be anything that you can't handle."

Brian still has doubts. During biblical times, prophets were always being killed and beheaded. Even Christ was crucified. But Lyla's words came from the heart, so he took them in the spirit that they were offered.

"Learn to 'Let go and let God.'"

"I will," he promised.

Even with his doubt, there was something beautiful about this moment. Their two spirits seemed to intertwine. From that point onward, he felt peaceful and strong. He felt united with God.

Lyla and Brian had enjoyed a special night. They danced so much that she had to take off her heels and put on a pair of tennis shoes. The wine relaxed them into their own little world. They spent the entire night touching, holding hands, and kissing. There was definitely something different going on. Intimacy had reached a feverish pitch. Even bringing up her mother didn't spoil the mood.

"My mother doesn't want you to know how happy she is about that lottery ticket," she explained.

"Oh yeah?" he smiled.

"It's not just about winning. Don't get me wrong; she loves winning. And she definitely loves money. But the two of you have a connection now. You're no longer just the guy stealing her daughter's attention away."

This was music to his ears. He tried his best to contain his enthusiasm - but couldn't.

"You know, Lyla," he said, taking her hands gently in mine. "If it *were* possible for me to steal *all of your attention*, I couldn't promise you that I wouldn't."

This didn't sound the way it sounded in his head. He was relieved to discover that something in the club had distracted Lyla at just the right moment.

"I'm sorry, Brian," she apologized. "What did you say?"

He wanted to get down on one knee and propose to Lyla that very second. The timing wasn't right, though. He pulled back, savoring the fresh urge to spend the rest of his life with his God-fearing princess. Beautiful, intelligent and humble; to him, Lyla was a woman on the cusp of greatness.

"I said I wanna lick you all over."

"Stop, Brian. You're gonna make me wet my panties."

He laughed happily.

"You should say that every day - *wet my panties*."

She bursts into laughter as the romantic mood transitions into a sexual, spiritual bliss.

He jumps into his car the very next day after work and heads to *Julian Jewelers* in Cleveland. There, he purchases a 2.17-carat diamond engagement ring for Lyla. A week later, they return to the same club where he decides that it was time to make his move. Lyla line danced to a couple of song while he ordered drinks. When she walks back to their table, he stands and pulls her chair out for her.

"Thank you, handsome!" she smiles, signaling for him to kiss her by tilting her head back.

Those juicy, red puckered lips look mesmerizing.

Sitting down, he feels a soft, warm palm on his left cheek. Sliding it to the back of his head, Lyla gently caresses his neck. His brain starts to tingle. This sensation shoots down from his neck to his elbows and lower back. Transfixed by this magical touch, he experiences a moment that his heart could reside in forever. It's time to get the ring ready, he decides.

On a pretend bathroom break, Brian retrieves it from the glove compartment of his car — excited like a little boy. There's no time to plan anything clever. In the midst of this enchanted atmosphere, he trusts that the right moment will present itself. Romance is at an extremely high pitch, and they haven't finished a single drink.

Returning to his seat, he takes a few seconds to bask in the knowledge that God has seen fit to bless him with such a divine companion. Beauty and humility are a powerful combination.

When the waiter leaves, he holds up his wine glass. Lyla responds by lifting hers and giggling. It's obvious that he's in a great mood.

"To the most beautiful woman in the world."

"Thank you!" she giggles again, before kissing him on the lips gently.

With no hint of what is about to happen, she finds humor in his ecstatic mood. Brian's younger brothers would say that he was being downright corny. But, if this is corny, then corny is something we should all cherish.

"I'm serious."

"Stop it, Brian. You're sexy when you're charming. Can't you tell that I've been a little high-charged since?"

"Yes! I love it!"

His heart is racing now. Realizing that this is the one moment in life that he grew up dreading, he pauses and takes a deep breath.

"As a matter of fact," he continues, dropping down to one knee.

Aware what is happening now, Lyla seems to be experiencing a mixture of emotions: happiness, surprise, and sadness. Brian reaches inside his jacket pocket and pulls out the ring. When Lyla sees it, she screams so loud that the other people in the club start to gather around. He's sweating bullets now. He's overwhelmed by the moment. His heart rate increases another beat as he places the ring on her finger. Lyla can't take it. Placing her free hand over her eyes, she begins to sob. When she finally removes it, her face is wet with tears.

'These are the best days of my life,' he realizes, looking up to thank God silently.

Looking at Lyla again, he finally asks her: "Will you marry me, Lyla Johnson?"

"Yes, baby," she says, wiping tears from her eyes. "Yes."

Leaning forward, she hugs him around the shoulder, kisses him on the lips, then looks square into his eyes. "Yes, baby, I will definitely marry you."

His mind goes blank in all the excitement. The crowd claps as the d-jay congratulates them and dedicates a song. Brian senses that the entire mood of the room has changed. Couples begin embracing romantically. Eyes closed and smiling slightly, he thinks to himself, 'feeling like this forever is what Heaven must be like.'

What a night!

Seeing his ring on Lyla's soft, beautiful hand was a sight for sore eyes. The next morning, they awaken; still on cloud nine.

Beginning with a soft knock on the door, however, events would escalate so quickly that the next few months is still a blur.

"Open up, Mr. Washington. We know you're in there."

Before Lyla and Brian can figure out what's happening, they hear a loud sound. Seconds later, four men wearing identical black suits rush into the bedroom. Pistols drawn, they surround the bed. Fearing for their lives, Lyla and Brian vaguely remember hearing the words *"Department of Homeland Security."*

Chapter 6

Lottery Interrogation

Sitting behind a gray marble desk holding a manila folder is 56 year old Colonel Taylor. He is dressed in full military uniform and wears a crew cut. With the exception of a mustache, he has no facial hair.

"Hello, sir," Brian greets Colonel Taylor respectfully before sitting.

Holding the manila folder up high, as though scanning a menu, Colonel Taylor doesn't respond. This goes on for almost ten minutes. 'If this is designed to piss me off,' Brian thinks to myself; 'it's working.' He had done nothing wrong. But, with a few deep breaths, he calms himself down. Colonel Taylor obviously wants to demonstrate his control. And, at the moment, he has all of the power. Thinking of how Lyla might handle this anger-provoking situation, he sits quietly and prays that God is with him.

At one point, a second officer comes in and hands Colonel Taylor a piece of paper that appeared to be related to a more important matter. Obviously startled, he makes a phone call; still refusing to acknowledge Brian's presence.

Waiting patiently, Brian coaches himself silently; under no illusion that the *Department of Homeland Security* gives a damn about his health or his safety. Entering the new millennium, America's vast wealth and military might had spoiled its greedy upper class. Under their leadership, the country was led astray spiritually. A spiritual correction was necessary to restore harmony and balance. This correction, Brian feared, came in the form of the 2020 version of the *Department of Homeland Security*. A rogue element in the department had metastasized under the leadership of Defense Secretary Robert Murphy. A more oppressive form of fascism had taken hold of the American government but not of the hearts and minds of the American people. Rather than dividing and lashing out at each other as they had done in the past, the citizens held together. Modern-day Babylon was in danger of falling; though not without bloody and costly battles.

Well into the 1980s, White men appeared to be at the top of America's ungodly food chain. It didn't seem to matter whether they were poor or wealthy. But during a betrayal of biblical proportions, the country's conservative leadership brazenly began shipping manufacturing jobs overseas. The hardworking blue-collar class was so mesmerized by former President Reagan's charisma and bravado that they failed to grasp the significance of his labor, tax and foreign policy.

For white, blue-collared males, the exodus of high-paying jobs had the stench of betrayal all over it. Having lured poor, white men into group-worship rather than God-worship, conservative leaders savored the moment that the trap shut down across their necks.

The centuries-old promotion of false religions and idolatry had played a major role in dividing the people.

A homeless woman once told Brian:

"Love God; but hate religion because religion leads to division. Where there's division, there's chaos. And where there's chaos, the devil sows seeds of destruction."

Staring deep into Colonel Taylor's cloudy, gray eyes, Brian was tempted to agree with her. While the American people were resting their own eyes, something in the government had gone terribly wrong.

All of Heaven was watching.

Finally, Colonel Taylor speaks. Skipping the greeting, he gets straight to the point.

"Do you know what an experienced lottery player does when he or she wants to bet ten dollars on a single three-digit number, Mr. Washington?"

Brian is surprised, and little alarmed, when Colonel Taylor mentions the lottery tickets. Apparently, the American military is light years ahead of everyone else when it comes to recognizing psychological profiles. Colonel Taylor seemed to enjoy using the phrase "different types." He used it over and over. Certain types ("non-players with inside information"), he explained, had a tendency to do exactly what Brian did.

"They go from not playing the lottery at all to betting as if they'd seen the winning number inside a crystal ball."

"It also doesn't occur to us," he explains with an accusative smile, "to purchase tickets for more than a dollar."

"Some people are just used to buying one dollar tickets."

Colonel Taylor pauses as if waiting for a confession. Though there is some truth to what he is saying, this sounds just a bit racist. Nevertheless, Brian holds his tongue.

"I'm willing to bet that your *momma* bought a lot of one dollar lottery tickets, Mr. Washington."

Pausing, Brian tries his best to not perceive this remark as disrespect aimed at his mother. He feels his blood pressure rising. The temptation to defend his mother's honor is too strong.

"What kind of tickets did *your momma* buy, Colonel Taylor?"

Colonel Taylor had armed men spread throughout the building. But no one was close enough to keep Brian from slamming him on his head if that's what he chose to do.

After a brief stare down, Colonel Taylor repeats the original question in a more threatening tone.

"Let me repeat the question again, Mr. Washington: Do you have any idea what an experienced lottery player would do if they suddenly felt the urge to bet ten dollars on a single lottery number?"

Still irritated, Brian is tempted to ask if the question is multiple-choice. But he decides against providing him with the motivation to demonstrate an inordinate amount of power. Reminding himself that Vice President Dick Cheney once shot a guy in the face without anyone even bothering to investigate the incident, he decides to stand down. Alienating Colonel Taylor further simply isn't worth the risk. Brian can already hear Lyla scolding him like a little boy for getting himself exiled to Guantanamo Bay.

"Don't you think you're taking this profiling thing too far? There's tens of millions of experienced lottery players, Colonel Taylor. We use a variety of methods to play the lottery."

Examining Brian's eyes closely, Colonel Taylor ponders this suggestion for a few seconds before responding.

"What method did you use in choosing to purchase your ten tickets, Mr. Washington?"

This deal about the ten one dollar tickets is nerve-wrecking, but Brian refuses to show fear. By now, he'd admitted to himself that purchasing ten one dollar tickets was a huge mistake. In his defense, he didn't see it as a matter of national security at the time at the time of the purchase.

Aware that he has Brian in a box, Colonel Taylor continues to press the issue.

"What type of player buys ten one dollar tickets – out of the blue?"

There was that word "type" again.

"A player who wants to give one dollar tickets to ten people?"

This sounded good in Brian's head, but not so good crossing his lips. Picking up on this slight chink in the armor, Colonel Taylor sits back in his chair and folds his arms. Brian manages to maintain his composure, but he realizes that no matter what he says or does, the question that he secretly dreads is coming.

"Is that what you did? Give the tickets away to everybody?"

Finally accepting the fact that this suggestion sounds ridiculous, Brian hedges his bet.

"Not all of them..."

When a huge smile suddenly appears on Colonel Taylor's face, it unnerves Brian. At any moment, he expects Colonel Taylor to ask how many tickets he kept for himself, and Brian is not sure what the answer will be. Heart racing now, he feels his facial muscles tightening. His mouth begins to feel dry. Colonel Taylor leans forward, leans back again, shifts his head to the right, then back to the left; still smiling.

"You got a number, yet?"

"What do you mean?"

Colonel Taylor's smile widens.

Reaching into his top, right desk drawer, he produces a white, porcelain bowl. It has small, square pieces of paper in it. Setting the bowl in the center of the table, Colonel Taylor instructs Brian to pick a piece of paper and read the number on it.

This is not good. Colonel Taylor had him outfoxed long before Brian entered his office. 'But of what crime was I guilty? How could any prove that I had dreamed up the winning lottery number?' Brian thought to himself. In this case, however, knowing it was just as serious a matter as proving it.

"I'm not in the mood for games, Colonel Taylor."

Hearing this, Colonel Taylor engages in a series of head gestures, drawing his thin lips in and out a few times. Reverting to the calm, flat tone with which he began the conversation, he asks a more ominous question.

"Are you in the mood for prison, Mr. Washington?"

"Why would the *Department of Homeland Security* be sending me to prison?"

"I could send you to prison for any number of reasons, including the failure to cooperate in a matter of national security."

"What matter of national security?"

Brian feels the box that Colonel Taylor has him in is getting tighter. 'This is crazy,' he thinks to himself. He can't believe that this asshole is talking about sending him to prison. 'Where is Lyla's God when I need him?' he thinks to himself.

Reluctantly, Brian chooses a piece of paper from the bowl. It's a three.

"Is that how many tickets you kept for yourself? Three?"

Still unable to decide, Brian hesitates before attempting to avoid the question.

"Is this what the *Department of Homeland Security* does? I wouldn't mind working here myself? If I guess the right number, do I win a prize?"

The Colonel stops smiling, unfolds his arms and leans forward with an angry scowl on his face. Intense and serious now, he lays it out for Brian.

"I'm asking a simple question, Mr. Washington."

Colonel Taylor is shouting now.

"What type of person," he continues, speaking slowly, as if this will aid Brian's understanding of the question, "buys ten one dollar lottery tickets instead of one ten dollar ticket? That's the *same* question we asked ourselves when we tracked the *first* little asshole that tried this trick. You know what we told ourselves? That it has to be somebody who lacks experience playing the lottery but - for some reason - is suddenly feeling very lucky. What can make a man feel that lucky, Mr. Washington?"

At a loss for words, Brian opens his mouth to speak but nothing comes out. Colonel Taylor continues, his voice growing louder with each question.

"Or better yet, what would make an otherwise intelligent man sit in the *Department of Homeland Security* and tell a simple-minded, bald-face lie? We have the videotape of you cashing in *all ten* lottery tickets."

He leans back and folds his arms again, shaking his head in disgust.

"What would make a man that confident; I mean, being so inexperienced and all?"

"Who says I'm inexperienced."

Genuinely tickled now, he smiles - in a manner foreboding evil.

Brian begins to realize that they have a pretty iron-clad case against him, but he didn't know what they wanted. If they wanted to ship him off to Guantanamo Bay, there was nothing that anyone could do to stop them. They had obviously interrogated the store owner. Yet, Brian saw no upside to confessing. Instead, he prayed silently that the powerful, faithful companion would rescue him from a situation that was dangerous and completely beyond his control. Making matters worse, he feels a bowel movement coming.

"I have to use the bathroom."

Overcome with laughter now, Colonel slaps the desk hard. His thunderous roar can be heard halfway down the long, marble hallway.

"You go right ahead, mister" he says, leaning forward again. "But don't you move from that goddamn chair."

For a moment, Brian feels startled. But the ridiculousness of the situation suddenly becomes clear. Crossing his hands, he leans forward.

"I'm not sure what sort of fascist country you think we live in," he says, angry enough to no longer give a fuck. "But this is the fuckin' United States of America."

His eyes look like they're about to pop out of their sockets.

"You know what this country's motto is?" Brian continues. "In God we trust."

Brian stands, slowly.

"So while I'm walking to the bathroom, you might wanna ask yourself a question that will put the rest of this bullshit in perspective."

Speaking slowly, he walks towards the door.

"To help me achieve the proper perspective, Colonel Taylor, my girlfriend constantly quotes a line about *loyalty* from a Mel Gibson movie."

Continuing the defiant act of approaching the door, he was a little surprised that Colonel Taylor didn't pull out his pistol or call for help. So angry that he didn't even bother to turn around, he asks the question that he'd been dying to ask this unworthy asshole:

"It must be great to have all this power. You undoubtedly feel a sense of personal accomplishment and purpose. Let me ask you this, though: Is *your* loyalty to the Gentleman *hanging on the cross* - or to the assholes *banging in the nails*? Given what you seem to be implying about my purchase of the lottery tickets, maybe you should ponder that question while I use the bathroom."

Although, Brian butchered the quote with by adding profanity and changing it into a question, Colonel Taylor seemed intelligent enough to get the gist of it.

Making it a single step beyond the door, he realizes that something is wrong with Colonel Taylor. Turning around and re-entering the room to get a closer look, he notices what turns out to be a *medicated needle* sticking out of his neck. He's almost three steps inside when Colonel Taylor's upper torso collapses like a rag doll. His forehead hits the desk so hard that it startles Brian. *He looks dead*.

"What the fuck is going on?" he ponders loud enough to be heard by anyone around.

Unsure what to do, he moves quietly towards to the door and peaks into the hallway. It's still empty. He has to get out of there, he decides. Playing it cool, he manages to get past the first door without catching anyone's attention. But there's another room, filled with people, between him and the stairs. Luckily, their backs are to him, except for the speaker; who seems preoccupied with his subject matter. Heart-racing, he manages to pass the room without capturing anyone's attention. He heads for the stairs, tip-toeing just in case someone is guarding it. On the first floor now he notices the security guard lying on the ground.

"This is strange," he mutters to himself. "First the dreams, now this."

"Psst!" he hears someone hiss. "Psst!"

Turning towards the sound; he laid eyes on Sis. Agnes for the very first time. 'This day just keeps getting crazier,' he remembers thinking. He just knows that this nun did not disable two members of the Office of Homeland Security with medicated needles. He tells himself, 'Maybe I'm dreaming again.'

"This way!" she says, whispering loudly.

He's not sure if he should trust her, but what other choice does he have? After all, she is wearing a nun costume.

"God, I hope you're with me right now," he says aloud, sighing.

He follows closely behind Sis. Agnes; moving quietly but rapidly.

"Who are you?" he asks.

"Sis. Agnes. A pleasure to meet you."

"Thanks for rescuing me. I'm Brian Washington."

"We know all about you, Mr. Washington. Why do you think we're here?"

"Who is *we*; if you don't mind me asking?"

"Let's talk later," she cuts him off abruptly, "follow me."

Exiting the building without arousing suspicion, they cross the street and enter the back seat of a car driven by another nun. A third nun is in the front passenger seat. As soon as they're inside, the driver pulls off. Looking back towards the building, it appeared as though the escape hasn't been detected, yet. Stressed beyond belief, he feels a throbbing sensation in his forehead. But, more than anything, he feels confused and agitated. Closing his eyes and praying that his head will stop spinning, he rests his forehead against his left palm. For some reason, his mind focuses intensely on the pressure that his left elbow exerts against his left thigh. This slows the spinning some. Heart still racing, he begins taking deep breaths in an attempt to regain his composure.

"Can somebody please tell me what's going on?" he mutters.

"Listen to me closely, Brian," Sis. Agnes begins. "Please accept my apology..."

"For what?"

With this, she jabs him in the left thigh with a medicated needle.

"Ouch!" he yells.

Looking over to complain to Sis. Agnes, he sees two of her, then three. He must have passed out shortly afterwards.

Two hours later, he's awakened by the sweet smell of apple pie.

"Somebody put their foot in that shit," he mutters incoherently, thinking he's at Lyla's.

Stumbling into the kitchen, he feels unusually groggy. But, as soon as he sees the three nuns, the events of the day rush back into his conscious mind.

"Did one of yall inject me with something?"

The three look at each other as if they don't know what he is talking about. A second later, Sis. Agnes raises her hand slowly. With a strange smile, she confesses.

"Sorry."

"Look lady, I can't remember your name right now. But can we agree that you won't be sticking me with anything. That is, if I ever have the misfortune of running into you again?"

"Misfortune?"

"Trust me," he says, remembering flashes of the previous night. "It's been a very unfortunate day. Where is Lyla?"

Looking back, it occurs to Brian just how groggy and grumpy he had to be to verbally attack a nun whose only crime was rescuing and demonstrating concern for his abnormally high stress level.

"We don't know where Lyla is," one of the other nuns answers. "We're having a difficult time locating her."

As soon as she says this, it occurs to Brian that they shouldn't even know who Lyla is.

"By the way, Mr. Washington," Sis. Agnes injects, "we're agreed on the needle thing. And you're free to go."

Jeff Mixon

Walking briskly, he heads towards the door; stopping when it occurs to him that the men from the *Department of Homeland Security* might be at Lyla's house waiting for him. he also realizes that he doesn't have a phone. The nuns remain silent, though, barely containing their amusement. They think he needs their help, and they're right.

"Let me ask you something Sis. Agnes – or maybe I should just call you Wonder Woman."

Brian hesitates for a moment to get his thoughts together as the nuns wait patiently.

"Actually, I have a question and a request."

"Anything you need, Mr. Washington."

Slightly amused now by the situation, Brian requests the use of a phone to call Lyla.

He considers letting his guard down for a moment. But, something holds him back. He should have felt grateful. But, racial tensions were high back in Cleveland, after three separate incidents of white police officers police beating unarmed black men to death surfaced on social media within a 48 hour period. It seems sort of stupid now, but he had a visceral reaction to being jabbed in the leg with a needle by a white woman that he didn't know.

The fact that Brian has an unusually strong fear of needles may have also played a role in his reaction.

"You seem to have a pretty good understanding of what's happening to me. How?"

Without saying a word, the three nuns continue smiling. In a matter of seconds, though, the answer becomes crystal clear.

"I get it. You know about me because the *Department of Homeland Security* knows about me. You've found a way to spy on them. Are you three really nuns?"

"Yes, we are. But, our mission is a little different."

Nothing else needed to be said. This moment of clarity changes things for some reason. Part of the reason that he was freaking out was because he didn't know what was happening.

"Do you know about the dream?"

They shake their heads up and down in unison.

"And you know about Lyla?"

"Yes, Brian," Sis. Agnes answers as the other nuns look on. "Congratulations on your engagement."

Jeff Mixon

"Ladies, I should thank you for helping me today. It was a tough day. I wish that I was still dreaming. But, even my dreams have been giving me trouble."

"Excuse me ladies," Sis. Agnes says.

The ladies exit, as Sis. Agnes takes Brian to the side. She is no longer smiling.

"Brian," she asks, looking worried now. "I sense that you're unwilling to accept our help. Why?"

"I'll be honest with you, Sis. Agnes. There's something inside of me that doesn't want to accept your help. Maybe, it has something to do with you jamming that needle in my leg."

"I'm sorry, Brian. You looked like you needed to relax. If you..."

Raising his left hand, he cut her off.

"Sis. Agnes, I don't want to accept your help, but I will. I have to because of Lyla. I'll work out my emotions later. Right now, though, I need to do what's necessary."

Sis. Agnes' sentimental smile makes him feel uncomfortable.

"The phone is through that door and to the left," she says, sensing his discomfort.

He becomes even more alarmed when Lyla doesn't answer the phone. Maybe upon discovering his escape, they went back to her house. But, why wouldn't they let her answer the phone?

He calls her again, but the phone just ring; causing him such agony that he had to use the bathroom again. He held out as long as he could.

"Come on, baby. Answer the phone."

Brian had to use the bathroom so badly now that he is forced to give up trying to contact Lyla; for now, but not for long.

"Fuck! Why did I have to buy all those stupid lottery tickets," he yells, almost in tears.

But there was little time for sorrow or regret.

Within a matter of hours, Sis. Agnes and the nuns discovered that Lyla was hiding out at her brother's place in Chicago. When she called him, Pastor Ricky had insisted that she leave with him.

Pictures of Lyla and Brian were plastered all over the television and internet. Nevertheless, Sis. Agnes managed to sneak him out of the house at night and drive him to Chicago.

Brian was relieved to see Lyla, but the fearful look in her eyes scared him.

"Baby," she says, hugging and kissing him, "I was worried to death about you. I kept crying and crying, but Ricky wouldn't let me call you."

Lyla sounded so pathetic that his attention shifted to her needs. For a few hours, he was able to stop worrying about the *Department of Homeland Security*.

"Lyla," he says, lifting her face from his wet shoulders so that he could see her eyes, "It's okay, baby. I understand that God is using us. This is amazing. I feel a deep sense of obligation to put my worries asides. I feel so honored; even though, unlike you, my name was chosen by some cosmic random number generator."

She laughs briefly, making him feel a little better. Taking her to the upstairs bathroom, he wipes the tears from hers before moving to her bedroom.

"No matter what happens to me, Lyla," he continues, once inside, "it was worth it to spend one second with you. Because of you, I feel worthy of being a soldier in God's army."

"Brian, don't talk like that. You talk like something bad is about to happen."

"I didn't mean it like that, Lyla," he says, attempting to put her mind at ease. "We can handle this mission. I even think that Colonel Taylor will be more reasonable in the future. How else can I write my book?"

Eager to switch topics, he remembers something important that he needs to share with Lyla. Holding his head downward to gather his thoughts, he begins slowly.

"Lyla," he pauses for another second. "I was freakin' out a little in the car, so Sis. Agnes jabbed me in the leg with a needle to make me fall asleep."

"She was just trying to help, baby," she says, resting her right cheek against his chest. "I love these big chest muscles."

"Feel free to rest against them any time you want. I work out just for you, baby. But, I need to tell you something."

Still not completely serious, Lyla gives Brian a peck on the lips, slowly and sensual this time.

"Go ahead, baby. What do you need to tell me?"

As soon as he begins to talk, though, Lyla interrupts again.

"Hold on, Brian. I'm sorry."

Beginning to feel a little impatient, he resists the temptation to become irritated with a woman possessing so much inner beauty - such faith in God - that the seriousness of the moment hasn't completely rattled her.

"I just want to tell you one thing, first."

"And what would that be, my beautiful princess?"

"I wanted to tell you how much I missed you. But, tell me what happened... *while you were asleep.*"

Based on her facial expression, it has finally struck Lyla that, typically, not a lot of things happen to a person while he's sleeping. Mouth wide open, she struggles to articulate her thought. He finishes it for her.

"Lyla, I had another dream."

Lyla was listening carefully now, so he continued.

"I'm gonna write a book one day called *Revelations*. I know that using that title sounds a little arrogant, even blasphemous; but that's what the dream showed me."

Suddenly, he thought of something that made him laugh.

"Oh yeah. I probably shouldn't tell you this until after we're married. But, I was bald in the dream."

Lyla couldn't help laughing at this. Looking up at his hair, she caresses his scalp gently with all five finger tips.

"Baby, I hate to tell you this, but you're almost bald already. Your hair is not quite a quarter inch long."

"Goodness," he exclaims, shaking his head while laughing. "Baby, my hair is the length that I instruct my barber to cut it. I could grow an afro in a month if I wanted. You'd better leave me alone. You know that I'm a soldier in God's army now."

Lyla smiles at this.

Grabbing Lyla around her tiny waist with just his hands, he slips further into play mode.

"Don't make me have to deal with you," he jokes, head-butting her gently.

"Mr. Washington," she replies with a sly smile, "you can deal with me any time you want."

When Lyla's brother enters the room, however, they freeze. For a few seconds, he regret leaving the door open.

"Here's your phone," Pastor Ricky says, extending it towards Brian.

The expression on his face is more serious than normal; something that Brian didn't think was possible.

"I left Lyla's phone at the house."

"Thank you," Brian says, noticing that the battery has been disconnected.

"That thing is a GPS device," he continues.

"I know."

"I didn't think they realized that your phone was missing, but they might be trying to track you now. Don't put the battery back in. I purchased three new phones for us to use for the time being. Right now, though, we should only call each other. I programmed Sis. Agnes' number into my phone in case we need her."

"Why couldn't you take my battery out?" Lyla injects in a manner typical of a little sister.

"We don't want them to know that you possess even a small amount of sophistication or to suspect that you're being helped by someone that does. According to Sis. Agnes, they know about Brian's spiritual gift but not yours."

For some reason, Brian feels the need to add his two cents.

"Relax, baby," he says, grabbing one hand gently. "Your brother's effort did the trick. People make mistakes in the fog of war."

Brian looks at Pastor Ricky, feeling very appreciative towards him.

"This one was minor. Calling him, however, would have been a huge mistake; the same mistake I made in attempting to call you."

Touched by the moment, Lyla hugs Brian and gives him a peck on the lips before leaving him to hug her brother.

"I'm sorry, Ricky. I guess I can still be a brat. You always protect me. You're the best big brother in the world."

Sensing that the moment was right for Lyla and her brother to spend some quality time together, Brian makes up an excuse to exit the bedroom.

"I have to pay the water bill," he says, before leaving.

Walking away, he makes a firm decision to pull Ricky to the side at the first opportunity. Brian wants to tell him how much he appreciates him. In his opinion, he couldn't have picked a better brother-in-law. He admires the way that he looks out for Lyla. Although he has moved to Chicago, he makes it to Akron in the drop of a hat whenever he senses that Lyla needs him.

Brian enjoys his conversation with Pastor Ricky. They share a beer. Brian even has the opportunity to see him laugh.

They grew closer during this period, something that would help their mission. Pastor Ricky had often referred to an outpouring of God's spirit, but there was little to give meaning or context to what was happening. That changed when Lyla's prophetic powers began to zero in on Cardinal Bell.

Chapter 7

Pope Under Fire

That night Brian had another dream. He wanted to tell Lyla about it when he awakened. But, sitting up in bed already, it was obvious that she was distracted.

A story broke on *Sixty Minutes* implicating Pope Francis in the decades-old pedophile priest scandal. Out of the blue, with no knowledge of the situation whatsoever, Lyla is adamant in her declaration that Pope Francis has been framed. Brian knows plenty of people who get a charge out of making this type of pronouncement, feigning sophistication. But, this wasn't consistent with Lyla's character. Normally deliberative and humble when it came to sensitive matters, she became very feisty.

"Lyla," Brian said calmly, waiting to get her attention.

"What?!"

"I believe you. But why are you so excited? This isn't like you."

"Because he's innocent!" she says, finally realizing that she's gotten beside herself.

"Okay."

Lyla's anger seems to be directed at Brian now.

"Forget it, Brian!"

When she gets out of the bed and starts to walk away, he grabs a wrist gently.

"Let go of me!"

Deciding that she needs a little space, he lets go.

For the rest of the day, Lyla is in a focused, distant mood. They talk, coordinating their activities for the next couple of days. But, it's easy too see that she lacks her usual animation. Worried about her, Brian decides not to bother her with the dream. Pastor Ricky was already at church. But, when Sis. Agnes pops up at the house unannounced, Brian tells her about the dream immediately.

"Why didn't you tell me?" Lyla asked, as though feeling betrayed.

Standing behind her, he gestures to Sis. Agnes in frustration. When she turns around, catching him, he tries to play it off with a serious answer.

"You were too busy watching coverage of the Pope Francis scandal when I tried to tell you this morning."

Lyla gives him a quick punch to the stomach. Sis. Agnes, meanwhile, exhibits little patience for their squabbling.

"What did you see?" she asks.

He had to ignore Lyla, accepting the fact, by now, that she became more feisty every time she saw one of the parties involved on television.

"I saw Amelia Bradford... on a computer... at a library."

"The library?" Lyla exclaims, thinking aloud. "That's strange."

"Why so?" Sis. Agnes asks.

"Because Amelia has a smart phone and personal computers with internet service at home and at work."

"Maybe she likes libraries," Brian suggests, dumbfounded.

"Or," Sis. Agnes jumps in, "Maybe she was sending a message that she couldn't chance being traced."

She turns to Brian.

"Think carefully, Brian. Did you see anything else?"

"Hold on. Give me a second."

Replaying the dream in his head, he realizes that nothing stood out about it until he saw Amelia Bradford. He was in the DVD section with his friend Milton who he hadn't seen in years. Had anyone else been sitting at the computer station he probably wouldn't have even remembered it.

"No," he tells them. "I just saw Amelia sitting at a computer terminal. I had a clear shot of her face but couldn't see what was on the monitor. I could tell that she was typing, even though I couldn't see her hands."

He thought for a few more seconds.

"There was one other thing."

"What?"

"She left fast."

Neither of them seemed to be impressed by the amount information the dream provided. Brian felt a little disappointed, too. Maybe it was just a random dream. If it wasn't, though, it had to provide a piece of useful information that they, that he, had overlooked.

As Lyla and Sis. Agnes continued mulling over its meaning Brian sat down and closed his eyes. The conversation grabbed his attention again when he heard Sis. Agnes says:

"The dream leads us to at least two questions. To whom did Amelia Bradford send the message? And why haven't they come forward?"

"If the message was about Marquis Daniels' kidnapping," Lyla asks, "why not send it to straight to the media? Or go to the police?"

Jumping back into the conversation, Brian explains: "I don't think that Marquis had been kidnapped, yet. I think he was shipped away *after* they discovered that Amelia was onto them."

"What makes you say that?"

"She would have gone to the police if Marquis had already been kidnapped. Otherwise, she would have become an accessory after the fact."

"So, why..." Sis. Agnes says, wandering to the other side of the room, "why would you have a dream that shows Amelia Bradford in the library on a computer... then running away?"

The room was silent for a few seconds before the answer became obvious to every one.

Jeff Mixon

"We don't have to answer all these questions, do we?" he said, observing their excited reactions.

"No, we don't," Sis. Agnes smiles.

"All we have to do," Lyla jumps in, excited now, "is find whatever it is that Amelia left somewhere for someone to find when the time was right. Amelia Bradford knew that we would be coming because..."

They waited for Brian to finish the thought.

"... because Marquis Daniels saw us coming."

They felt better now that they had figured out a key piece of the puzzle. They could now begin to speculate about how they might find the next piece.

"I have a friend," says Sis. Agnes, "who should be able to provide us with Amelia's library card number and track her internet activity in the weeks leading up to her murder."

Taking out his new phone, Brian links onto the registration page of the most popular social media website of the day - *CURRENT*.

"What are you doing, Brian?" Lyla asks.

"Starting a fake *CURRENT* account. Something tells me that among Amelia Bradford's *CURRENT* videos we'll find a video of Marquis Daniels predicting that rainbow - a *time-stamped* video. That would expose Bishop Matthias as a fraud and blow the entire Levin-Matthias plan out of the water."

"It sure would. Good idea."

"I have to become friends with her first," he said, typing with both thumbs.

"Yeah. But she's dead. How can she friend you back?"

"On *CURRENT*, if you don't reject a friend request it goes through automatically after three days."

"That's right!"

Shortly after Sis. Agnes finished with her phone call, he sent the friend request.

"What now?" he asks.

"We need to get back to Ohio."

Chapter 8

Men In Black

Pastor Ricky, Sis. Agnes and Brian agreed that he should go back to Ohio with her alone. Lyla would stay in Chicago. This irritated her to no end, of course.

After Pastor Ricky gave Lyla and Brian the cell phones he made them promise not to call anyone except each other. Without mentioning it to him, Brian took this to mean that they shouldn't call anyone with which they were *known* to associate. That didn't include his friend Eric from college. He needed someone who knew how to hack a computer. After yet another dream, he made the decision to call Eric without informing the others.

Overshadowed by the media's fascination with the Pope Francis scandal and "unnatural threats to the safety and security of the United States of America," which was a seemingly unrelated story, it caught Brian's attention initially because it took place in his hometown. A worker at a Cleveland orphanage, Amelia Bradford, had been found murdered amid rumors that an orphan boy, Marquise Daniels, had vanished. Remembering

Jeff Mixon

Lyla's off-handed comment about the true predictor of the rainbow being kidnapped or dead, Brian's mind kept connecting the two stories. Lyla's statement had stuck in his mind. This most recent dream provided theoretical details that allowed him to piece together a working hypothesis.

The dream clearly suggested that upon discovering Marquise's ability to prophesy, Peter Levin's crew kidnapped him then killed the only person who knew about his rainbow prediction, Amelia Bradford. The rainbow prediction became the centerpiece of a plot to take control of the Vatican. But, how could Lyla and he prove that Amelia and Peter even knew each other? When Brian called Lyla to get her opinion on the matter, she drew a blank. Nevertheless, he became even more intrigued by her revelation of a scandal involving Father Donovan and Peter Levin. Unable to let it go, he called the one person he knew who might be able to shine light on the subject. His college roommate and fraternity brother Eric was not only a detective; he was, in some circles, a well-known computer hacker. After checking out Eric's website he knew that the subject matter was way too juicy for him to pass up before getting a few details. Brian offered none. He probed, instead, to see if he was familiar with Peter Levin.

"The CEO of Chevron Oil?" Eric asked.

The inflection in his voice already showed interest.

"That's him," Brian replied. "What did you think about Bishop Matthias' rainbow prediction?"

"Dude, that was nuts. He had to use some kind of special effects machine or something."

"He's got a lot of people talking."

"I know. The Prophet Elijah! He's even got my mother believing that crap. I can't believe all those people getting sucked in. It's like Y2K all over again. This is the biggest con game in history. The entire universe is going nuts."

"What would you say if I told you that Peter Levin murdered that worker from the orphanage, Amelia Bradford?"

"I'd say run and hide. Any witness to that murder needs a pre-planned funeral package."

"Levin didn't physically murder her. According to my sources, though, he had her killed."

That was enough for now.

"Hey, I'm sorry Eric. I have an emergency."

"It was good hearing from you dude. Go easy with the conspiracy theories. Even if you knew what was going on, there's nothing anyone could do about it. Peter Levin has a license to kill."

Eric didn't really believe the part about there being nothing that anyone could do. With a laptop at his fingertips, he was capable of slaying even bigger giants than Peter Levin. He'd shown a little hesitation over the phone, but Eric lived for the type of scenario that was about to be delivered to his doorstep.

Still, Brian was surprised to receive a phone call from Eric the very next morning while cooking breakfast.

"Eric. Whassup?"

"Amelia Bradford."

"Oh yeah? What can you tell me about her?""

"She graduated from the same high school as Peter Levin. Get this. She was the head cheerleader the year that he led the football team to an undefeated season."

That sounded promising.

"How much do you wanna bet they partied together?"

"Hold on, Eric."

Brian takes a few seconds to flip three sausages so that the side touching the pan won't over cook while he's on the phone.

"Okay. Go ahead."

"I set up a couple of information channels after we spoke yesterday."

At this point, Eric begins talking so fast that Brian remains silent.

"Dude, what the fuck? How did you get this information? I don't even wanna know. I hope your life isn't in danger."

Brian was impressed with the information that Eric had shared, but annoyed that he kept saying:

"Dude, I hope your life isn't in danger."

"No, I think I'm okay. I got the information from somebody else."

"Dude, whoever it is. If the wrong person knows, that they know, their lives aren't worth two cents."

Brian's thoughts automatically turn to Lyla, but his faith in God was beginning to outweigh his anxiety.

Around 4:30 A.M. the next morning, Eric called with more news.

"Hey, buddy." Brian greets him, barely awake. "What you got?"

"Don't tell me you were asleep."

"It's 4:30 A.M."

"Dude, you're sleeping your life away!"

"Eric..."

"Okay, Sleepyhead. You ready?"

"Yeah."

"I discovered the dummy e-mail account that Peter Levin's right hand man, Tony Shanklin, is using to communicate with - *guess who*?"

It usually took at least one cup of coffee to unscramble his mind this early in the morning. Brian honestly had no clue who Eric was talking about.

"I don't know. The Pope?"

"No, stupid. The person holding Marquise Daniels!"

"The who?" Brian said, suddenly awake.

"And get this; you probably know the person."

"Who is he?"

"Who is *she*? Get this. *Dorothea Allred*."

"Dorothea Allred? *Are you sure?*"

From Brian's days as a resident of Cleveland's near west side, he was familiar with the name Dorothea Allred. She had won Ward 3's Senior of the Year Award numerous times. It was also widely rumored that she had used her position as president of the Local Advisory Council to extort resident drug dealers. According to the rumors, she used her power to influence the eviction process to take control of the drug trade at *Lakeview Estates*, but kidnapping?

"I don't know her, but I definitely know of her. She must be doing someone a huge favor."

"Dude, if a little African-American kid suddenly pops up in a Caucasian neighborhood, he sticks out like a sore thumb."

"You're right. In a low income, predominantly black high rise, he would blend right in."

"That's right, 2700 Washington Avenue, Apartment 1402."

"How did you find all this out?"

"They e-mail her using one of Tony Shanklin's dummy e-mail accounts and code words so obvious they're laughable."

"Wow, I have to admit it, Eric. I'm impressed. That was fast. *Thank you!* I owe you one."

Brian could almost see Eric's Double Expresso smile beaming through the phone.

"Wait until Lyla finds out!"

As soon as he mention Lyla's name he realizes that he'd made a mistake.

"Who's Lyla?"

Brian hesitates a second before answering.

"Another interested party."

It's pretty obvious to someone as sharp as Eric that Brian is avoiding the question. But, he doesn't pry.

That night, dressed in a brown hoodie and shades, Brian sneaks over to *Lakeview Estates* to do a little digging. A childhood friend, Hollywood, confirmed just about everything that Eric told him. According to her, Ms. Allred's *grandson* moved in with her about a month earlier. And, among other things – a mysterious white male visitor began hanging around the building and would even visit Ms. Allred from time to time. Moreover, when Brian downloaded a picture of Marquise Daniel from her computer, Hollywood confirmed that the young boy that she had seen in apartment 1402 was, indeed, Marquise Daniels.

Leaving *Lakeview Estates* turned out to be more adventurous than Brian had imagined.

Hollywood and Brian hadn't seen each other in years. She insisted that he hang out for a while so that they could catch up. Hungry, it was difficult to turn down a late night dinner, complete with peach cobbler and ice cream for dessert. He had forgotten how good of a cook she was.

After a couple of glasses of wine and a little reminiscing, he managed to relax for the first time since Sis. Ages stabbed him in the leg with the needle. He could not reveal too much information to Hollywood for fear that it might put her at-risk, but she got a huge laugh out of the story about how he reacted when Sis. Agnes stuck him with the needles. Hollywood was well aware of Brian's fear of needles, which went all the way back to childhood.

"I'm surprised you didn't kill her," she laughed.

The high rise at *Lakeview Estates* has gigantic windows, from waist-level to the ceiling, stretching from wall to wall. While enjoying the so-called million-dollar view – Lake Erie on one side and the downtown skyline on the other – Brian sees a gold Mercedes and another luxury automobile enter the parking lot simultaneously. Six men in suits exit the two vehicles. In the darkness it was hard to say for sure than they were from the *Department of Homeland Security*. The gold Mercedes threw him off, but he decided not to take any chances. There was too much at stake.

"I need to get out of here without anyone seeing me. I also need to avoid those four white men headed towards the front door."

For a minute, Hollywood seemed stumped. But, Brian sensed that she had figured out an escape route when a smile came over her face.

"What about the back patio? There's about a ten feet drop to the ground. Then you can come around the building and sneak into the parking lot."

"That's perfect," he says, hugging her and giving her a friendly kiss on the neck. *"Thank you!"*

"When everything cools down, come back and see me again."

"I will," he says, creeping over to the door. "I'm sorry I have to leave so fast, but I really need to get out of here before I get you into trouble."

But, as soon as he touches the door handle, they hear loud knocking. Seconds away from freaking out, judging by the look on her face, Brian quickly places his hand over her mouth.

"Relax," he whispers. "They don't know which apartment I'm in. I heard knocking next door thirty seconds ago. They're going door to door. Relax and breathe through your nose."

This seemed to calm her down some.

"They're probably about to leave," he assures her, still whispering. "That's it. Breathe through your nose. In a few minutes, I'm gonna sneak out of here without anyone seeing me."

They hear knocking at the next unit, then the next. They are also hearing the men talking to some of Hollywood's neighbors.

"Where can we meet tomorrow?" he asks when the hallway becomes completely quiet.

"At the Fulton Library, down the street."

"Is 10:00 a.m. Okay?"

"Okay, baby. Be safe."

"I will. I'll see you tomorrow at the Fulton Library - 10 o' clock."

"Okay."

He's not sure why he lied to Hollywood; but if he got out of this situation alive, he and Lyla would have to take her out to dinner.

From Hollywood's second floor window, he had seen four men head towards the building while two remained in the parking lot. There were two elevators and two stairwells. That would account for all four of the men inside the building. Assuming that they were working their way upwards, he eased over to the stairwell closest to the pool room to see if he could hear anything. They were definitely headed upwards, so he quickly descended the stairs to the first floor and headed to the patio. On his way, however, something alerts him to the danger at the back door. So, he decides to go through the pool room, instead, and hang jump from the window. When he opens the window, though, he hears one of the men talking on a walkie-talkie.

"You think we should give this little asshole enough time to say his prayers?"

"What for? So we can get hit by a lightening bolt? Shoot the bastard and call it a day. This whole situation creeps me out. All money ain't good money."

"It is where I come from."

Brian waits for him to return to the front of the building before he climbs out. Hanging from the window seal with just a two feet drop, he's careful to land on his toes. Wearing track shoes, he barely makes any noise. His car is located in the opposite direction of the front door. Staying low to the ground, he takes a roundabout route in order to avoid detection, but an elderly woman becomes startled when she sees him and starts screaming. Grabbing the keys from his pocket, he starts running towards the car; hitting the door lock with the remote.

Before they can alert the others, Brian jumps in the car and throws it in reverse. Without sufficient time to wait for the others, one of the agent runs towards the car. But, when he jumps out of the way to avoid being hit, Brian slams the car into drive and pulls out of the parking lot amidst heavy gunfire. From here, he makes one left turn and three right turns onto I-90 East, gambling that drivers unfamiliar with the area won't realize that they can beat him to the highway entrance ramp with a right out of the parking lot followed by a quick left.

Downloading Marquise Daniel's picture from the internet to an IP address located at *Lakeview Estates* was a huge mistake.

"No harm, no foul," he tells myself.

In the back of his mind, though, he realizes that even a small mistake is enough to get one of them killed. Not only does he tell Sis. Agnes and Lyla what happened, he promises them that he won't jeopardize any of their lives again by taking unnecessary risks. He considered himself fortunate to be alive and even more fortunate that his boneheaded mistake was overshadowed by the news that Eric had located Marquise Daniels.

Within an hour, members of the *Department of Homeland Security* pulled up to the safe house where Sis. Agnes and Brian were hiding out.

"They're here, Sis. Agnes," he yells, running down the stairs to the first floor so fast that he almost crashes into the wall at the bottom.

Sis. Agnes responds by quietly making a cross with her thin unpainted lip and an index finger. The fact that she remains calm has the effect of calming him down.

"They're not here to kill us, and they don't know that we know they're coming. Walk outside quietly with me as if we were already leaving, then follow my lead."

Once again, he trusts her.

"All we have to do is make it to the next safe house," she says, watching them exit two vehicles through a small opening in the curtains. "By now, they know we're involved. They simply refer to us as *The Nuns*."

Sis. Agnes waits patiently. She then instructs Brian to follow her. He begins taking deep breaths as they approach them, unaware that Sis. Agnes is already in ass-kicking mode.

Two men remain on the sidewalk next to the car while the other three approach them near the bottom of the steps. Removing their guns slowly, one of the three men approaching them tries to reason with Sis. Agnes.

"Be careful with the needles, Sister," one of them says. "We come in peace."

What happened over the next five minutes is still a blur.

They basically have three options: run, give up - or fight! On this particular day, Brian doubts that the first two options even occurred to Sis. Agnes.

Jeff Mixon

Kicking one of the men in the face with a lightening fast side kick, she knocks him out completely out. Then, reaching into her sleeves, she produces two miniature blow darts. She hits one man, causing him to collapse in a matter of seconds; but she misses the second man. *Surreal* doesn't begin to describe the scene taking place in front of him.

"What the fuck is this?" he says, stunned.

Sis. Agnes reaches down and grabs the man's testicles; squeezing them hard. Stepping back first, she then kicks him in the face – knocking him down. By now, the two men standing on the side walk are charging hard. Leaning back into a karate stance, Brian goes into fight-or-flight mode. As far as he's concerned, his life is on the line – and so is theirs!

One of the guys that Sis. Agnes knocked down stands up, grabbing her from behind. She head-butts him and kicks one of the other men.

Still outnumbered, Brian has no choice but to join the action.

He kicks one of them square in the face with a round house kick. A second guy gets caught with an elbow to the eye socket. When the first guy tries to stand up, Brian trips him, landing a side kick to his chin before he hits the ground. Obviously dazed, Brian finishes him off with another round. When two car loads of nuns brandishing blow darts pull up, the remaining men collapse like wets sacks of potatoes.

It wouldn't be long, he sensed, before gun play would be involved.

Speeding westward across the Detroit-Superior, Sis. Agnes and Brian notice a gold Mercedes following them. The driver is a young African-American woman. Instead of heading to their original destination, St. Malachi's, Brian passes West 25th, makes a right at West 28th and another right onto Washington Avenue. Turning left into the parking lot of *Lakeview Estates*, he parks. When Sis. Agnes and Brian see the gold Mercedes approaching, they get out and investigate; but the car speeds past them so fast that they're unable to get a good look at the driver. Brian's mind must be playing tricks on him. Although, he can't trace the train of thought that led him to this conclusion, his instincts suggest two things. Number one, the car is a rental car. Number two, Lyla's cousin Celeste was the driver. The problem with the second hypothesis is that, as far as he knew, Celeste was still in jail.

As if on cue, he receives a call from Lyla as he and Sis. Agnes made their way out of the parking lot onto the highway to the next safe house.

"Hey, baby. What's up?"

"Brian!" she says with a sense of urgency.

"Yes?"

"Listen to me, Brian. Wherever you are, you're close to Marquise Daniels."

"I know. I know exactly where Marquise is. Let me hang up and report it to the police. Then, I'll call you right back."

On the phone with a dispatcher from the Cleveland Police Department, Brian overhears Sis. Agnes' phone conversation.

"Get over to *Lakeview Estates*, 2700 Washington Avenue, just off Detroit. Keep an eye on things just in case they decide to move Marquise to a different location."

Both off the phone now, Sis. Agnes says something that surprises him.

"I don't think the men that showed up at the safe house are working with Peter Levin."

Intrigued by the statement, he asks, "How do you know?"

"Well, number one, that's not the way they operate. Number two, if those men were working with Peter Levin the two of us would be dead now."

This sounded ominous.

"The vast major of people at the *Department of Homeland Security* are conducting the crackdown without knowledge that anything nefarious is involved."

Brian had no way of knowing whether Sis. Agnes was right, but it sounded hopeful.

From his understanding of things, at least, the discovery of Marquise Daniels whereabouts changed the entire equation. The *Department of Homeland Security* was rounding up innocent people discovered to have been engifted by an outpouring of God's spirit. But, a rogue element, men connected to Peter Levin and Bishop Matthias, would now attempt to kill him. As far as this band of thugs was concerned, the moment that Brian was discovered to be in the *Lakeview Estates* parking lot he became public enemy number one.

As he prepared to turn in that night, something that Hollywood said surprised him.

"My friend, Brenda, thought that Dorothea Allred might be drugging him."

"Why would she think that?" Brian asked.

"Because he was always drowsy."

Sis. Agnes and Brian were happy to discover the next morning that Marquise Daniels was now safely in the hands of the police. Hearing this, he thought that the mission was over. But, Sis. Agnes quickly threw cold water on this suggestion.

"Our mission isn't over - nor are we safe - until the people behind the kidnapping are behind bars."

Chapter 9

On The Run!

After speaking to Colonel Taylor by phone, it was Sis. Agnes' idea to go dancing. Brian wasn't sure what this meant, though. Along with about a hundred other people, his face was still plastered over the news - morning, noon and night. Lyla placed an extreme level of trust in her for some reasons as though the two of them shared some secret to which he wasn't privy. Maybe, if he hadn't failed to mention the gunfire they would have come to a different decision. But, having covered it up initially so that Lyla wouldn't worry too much, he came to the conclusion that their lives would be in no more or less danger if he told them.

Brian continued to have moments of doubt.

But with each passing day, there were more and more moments when he truly believed that God - our powerful, faith companion - would see them through this extraordinary moment in their lives.

Sitting at the bar, sipping a Rum and Coke, Brian watched Sis. Agnes and Lyla perform like they were on a mission. It was fun to watch. Tossing their heads back in joy and unison, they read each others' movement; remaining in sync. Meanwhile, he was consumed by thoughts of the *Department of Homeland Security* busting through the door. He was simply too wound up to get into the swing of things.

No one knew where they were. The only cells phone that they had had never been used before. Sis. Agnes had even changed clothes. But, something about the way the hotel security officer studied Sis. Agnes' face when they left the hotel gave him an eerie feeling.

Eventually, he joined Lyla and Sis. Agnes on the dance floor. Lyla bailed him out after three songs, however, when she asked Brian to send a friend request to Marquis Daniels on his fake CURRENT account. It was as good an idea as any that they had come up with, so far. So, Brian left the crowded dance floor, headed back to his bar stool and sent the friend request. Before he could order another round of drinks, though, Lyla and Sis. Agnes made their way over to the bar.

"It's time to go," Lyla said nervously, looking towards the guys checking identification at the door.

When he looked over he saw three men in uniforms issued by the *Department of Homeland Security* talking to the door check guy.

"Did you send the friend request?" Lyla said impatiently.

"Yes."

"Good," she said, grabbing the phone from his hand. "We need to get rid of this."

One man did the talking. He appeared to be showing the guy at the door their photos, while the other two men looked around the club. They hadn't spotted them yet, though, in the dense crowd.

As with most clubs on the west bank of *The Flats* there were two ways to exit *Club Mega*. They could wait for the front parking lot entrance to clear and try to sneak out or they could take the *Lake Erie* exit. Since they didn't have a boat, he assumed that they'd try the first strategy. But Lyla, realizing how important it was to get rid of the phone, had other ideas.

"This way," she said, walking towards the glass doors leading out onto the dock.

As soon as they're outside, she flings the cell phone into the water.

"Now what?"

Again, he saw two choices. He was a terrible swimmer, so he decided to steal a boat. He came within seconds of commandeering a boat from two drunken passengers. Fortunately, Sis. Agnes pointed out a third option. They simply walked down the dock to *Club Paradise*, entered through the dock entrance and exited into the front parking lot. They were less than a mile away from *Lakeview Estates*, the low income housing units where Marquis Daniels had been held captive.

"How did they know we were here?" Lyla asks.

Walking briskly, the hotel security officer came to Brian's mind. But, it was just a hunch.

"I don't know."

It was while attempting to escape through the front parking lot of the west bank of *The Flats* that they first laid eyes on Father Donovan. The fatherly-looking, gray-haired priest would turn out to be anything but fatherly. First, they saw the hotel security officer, though; confirming his suspicion.

"There they go!" he said, pointing at them.

But when Father Donovan pulled a pistol from his inside coat pocket and pointed it in their direction, the officer attempted to stop him. Unfortunately, Father Donovan didn't hesitate to end his life with two shots from a pistol with a silencer. Horrified when he fell to the ground, Lyla stops momentarily. But, as grateful to Officer Timothy Bennett for risking his life to save theirs, there was nothing that they could do to save him. Brian couldn't bear watching Lyla get shot attempting to do so.

"Run!" he yells, grabbing her by the arm.

Running for their lives now, they heard two sounds that continued to give Brian occasional nightmares years later. The first sound was the sound of bullets bouncing off parked cars. The second sound was the loud footsteps of the three men they saw in the club. Judging by the sound, these men were moving so fast that Brian didn't see how all three of them could out run them. Lyla, a high school track star, was okay once he convinced her that she had to run as fast as she could so that he could focus on helping Sis. Agnes. Fortunately, a car bearing bright lights pulls into the parking, blinding them enough to force them to stop running. They heard one of them scream "fuck" when he made contact with a parked car.

"Thank you, Heavenly Father," Sis. Agnes exclaims, slowing down.

The shooting appeared to have stopped, but one of the men was still chasing us. Not for long, though. Sis. Agnes pulls a dart out of nowhere and launches it into his chest.

"Ah!" he yells, then stops to pull the dart from his chest.

"Let's go," Sis. Agnes says. "We won't have to worry about him for a while."

Sure enough, the man attempts to start chasing us again; but he stumbles and collapses after a few steps.

Brian can't believe his eyes.

"You're a dangerous woman," he says, running next to her.

They have no idea where Lyla is, however, until a car pulls up next to them and she yells, "Get in!"

The driver of the car is another nun.

"What took you so long?" Sis. Agnes asks, out of breath.

"You came out of the wrong door."

"Sorry. We were being chased. Thank you."

"Take your time and catch you breath," Lyla interjects. "Thank God nobody got hurt."

Breathing hard himself, Brian tries to figure out their next move.

"I don't think we should go back to the hotel," Lyla says, as if reading his mind.

"I agree."

"Don't worry," Sis. Agnes says, breathing almost normal now. "We know a safe place to hide."

They drove down Washington Avenue, taking a left onto W. 25 and a second left onto the Detroit-Superior Bridge.

"Stay on this street for twenty minutes," Brian informed them, "and we'll be in my old neighborhood."

The two nuns looked at each other and smiled. Twenty minutes later he understood the smiles when they pulled into the parking lot of the seminary on Ansel Road, where Brian played football and basketball as a child. Although the priests occasionally passed out brown bag lunches, children were never allowed inside. The basement of the building must have been remodeled. From there, it looked like a recently built structure. There must have been a hundred computers.

"Don't worry," Sis. Agnes says, giving them a tour, "electronic signals can't be traced to this location. It takes a little longer to log onto websites because internet traffic travels to a foreign IP address before it's re-routed to the target location. It's well worth it, though."

Lyla is in awe.

"Impressive!"

"The sisters wearing the headset constantly monitor for attempts to track our signal. Because the information travels such a convoluted route, they have sufficient time to intercept information about our location and replace it with bogus information."

"They transmit a fake IP address? Kind of like tricking caller ID," Lyla says, surprising Brian.

"Exactly."

"Let me show you something else," Sis. Agnes says, walking towards the other end of the room. "I guess if God trusts the two of you, we can."

Marching down a hallway the length of a city block, Sis. Agnes moves so fast that they could barely keep up. Unaware that she can still hear them, Lyla taunts Brian in a hushed voice.

"You didn't think I knew about computers, did you?"

"I plead the fifth."

"Smart man!" Sis. Agnes chimes in.

Brian smiles, gloating really.

"You didn't think she would hear you, *did you?*"

The look on Ms. Goody-Two-Shoes' face is priceless.

It takes almost five minutes to reach their destination. Traveling up the elevator to the first floor, they find themselves inside of Bethany Church on East 105th Street.

Looking out the church window, at a beverage store that Brian still frequents occasionally, Brian says: "Is someone planning a quick getaway?"

Sis. Agnes is suddenly very serious.

"True followers of our Lord and Savior have been persecuted since His birth."

As they reflect on the magnitude of the situation and its surrealism, the mood becomes quiet and somber. Brian never imagined an experience so humbling in all his life. For him, at least, it was impossible to feel worthy of this magnificent calling. In order to maintain cognitive balance he had to occasionally remind himself that "God doesn't pick the qualified; He qualifies the picked."

"So, what's our next move?" Brian asks, breaking the silence.

"For now, back to the computer lab. After the prayer session, I'll show the two of you where you'll be sleeping."

Before his brain could even translate the reaction of his sinful nature into words, Sis. Agnes splashes it with ice water.

"In separate quarters, of course."

Muffling his own disappointment, Brian looks at Lyla. She responds by ignoring him and changing the subject. But, he sees the disappointment in her face.

"Did either of you notice that the guy in the trench coat was the only one shooting at us?"

"Yes," Sis. Agnes says. "He must have come with them originally. But when they ran towards it, he quickly put the gun away."

"What do you make of that?" he asks.

"I'm not sure. But it's possible that we have potential allies in the *Department of Homeland Security*."

This is good news. Closing her eyes, Lyla raises both fists in the air.

"Praise the Lord!"

Looking at her watch, Sis. Agnes responds, "We'd better get to the computer lab. Prayer Session starts in forty-three minutes."

The session at the computer lab was impressive and revealing. Nevertheless, the wind was knocked out of their sails three days later when they discovered that there was nothing on Marquis Daniels' CURRENT timeline related to the rainbow prediction or Amelia Bradford's death. There were no videos at all.

"But, look at this," Lyla says.

Sis. Agnes and Brian ease a little closer to the monitor, looking over her shoulders.

"What is it?"

"The attendance sheet that I copied listed the names of nineteen orphans; Marquis and eighteen classmates."

"Okay…"

They wait for her to get to the point.

"Now, look at this."

Sis. Agnes and Brian move their faces closer, but he still can't read the screen.

"Can you just tell us what it says, Lyla?" he says, impatiently.

Sis. Agnes stops looking at the screen, turning to observe Brian squinting.

"Looks like somebody needs glasses."

Growing frustrated, he turns and stares directly into her eyes.

"No offense," she says, putting her reading glasses on, bending down to read what's on the screen.

"None taken," he says, struggling to keep his wits about himself.

Somehow this innocent moment, a moment of high expectations, turns into his personal little nightmare. He's risking his life to help someone he never met – and his two partners are making issue of his poor eyesight? He's being double-teamed by the *Righteous Sisters*.

"Pay attention, Brian!" Lyla demands.

"Please God," he says, lifting his eyes to the ceiling. "Help me."

When he returns his attention to the screen, there is a long gap in conversation.

"We're waiting on you, Brian. This is important."

"I'm listening, Lyla. I'm right *behind you*."

"Stop talking."

"I wasn't talking."

Sis. Agnes gets in on the act with a loud shushing sound.

"Shhhhh!"

'This is ridiculous,' he thinks to himself, agitated now. 'On what planet would I have to be the bigger person in a room with this God-fearing twosome? The Planet Earth, apparently.' Extremely irritated at the senselessness of the entire conversation, Brian takes a deep breath, counts to ten silently and calms down.

"I'm sorry. Please continue."

"Marquis Daniels has twenty friends," Lyla continues. "Eighteen classmates, Amelia Bradford and one more."

'Instead of just telling us the name of the mystery person,' Brian laments, 'here she goes with the suspense again.'

"Let me guess," he says, just so she can get on with it, "the Pope?!"

"No dummy!"

Sis. Agnes leans in closer and smiles.

"Your wife!"

Standing up straight, she looks at Brian; but he has no clue what she's talking about.

"Whose wife? I'm not…."

Lyla stands up, smiles and kisses him.

"What is this, the *Twilight Zone*? A second ago, you two were yelling at me. Now, it's all kisses and smiles."

Brian really could have used an *Advil* to deal with the headache they seemed intent on giving him. It was beginning to get on his nerves. A stiff drink and a nap couldn't have hurt.

"Sit down and take a look," Lyla says.

Sitting, he scans the friend list.

"Anything jumping out at you, Mr. Washington?"

That's when he sees a friend with the last name Washington. First name? Lyla.

"Wow! We do have a *powerful, faithful companion* – and a little human help. Thank you Marquis and Amelia!"

"Don't forget Sis. Agnes," Lyla says, hugging her. "We love you Sis. Agnes."

Brian takes a pass on the love fest taking place behind him, waiting to see what their next move is.

"Thanks to you too. We still haven't found a video, but I'm hopeful; hopeful enough to contact my friend Sis. Theresa of the *Associated Press*."

"There it is; a message to the *Associated Press*."

"Say no more Sis. Agnes. Let me find her name first, then I'll inbox her."

"What do you want the message to say?" Lyla asks.

On the same page with Sister Agnes now, Brian answers for her.

"She wants Sis. Theresa to send my beautiful wife a friend request. If we're right about Amelia Bradford hiding a video on her page, I mean, your page, the infamous Rainbow Caper will be exposed before the week is out. And I'm just about finished. There!"

He hits the SEND button.

"Message sent!"

Standing up, Brian gives Lyla an enthusiastic hug and peck on the cheek. She responds with a two second kiss on the mouth; the kind of kiss that could have easily ignited a moment of passion. When Sis. Agnes cleared her throat, however, all systems shut down.

"Sorry, Sis. Agnes," Lyla says. "It's been a while."

Lyla steps away from him. He can see how guilty she feels by the look on her face.

"Believe me, I understand."

Especially attractive for a nun, he wonders what she means by *I understand*. But, he manages to stay focused. This is as good a time as any to deal with some feelings that have been bothering him, so he asks to speak with Sis. Agnes privately.

"When you have a moment to spare I need to talk to you - alone."

As they both realize that by *alone* he means *without Lyla*, the moment becomes slightly awkward. He assumes that Sis. Agnes and he might go for a walk. Instead, Lyla decides that it's a good time to soak her sore muscles in a tub of warm water. He starts to call her back. But fear that he might not be able to overcome the temptation to censor himself in her presence prevents him from taking the risk.

"It won't take long, Lyla," he said, walking fast enough to beat her to the bathroom door.

He really didn't have a reason to believe that Lyla was bothered by his desire to talk to Sis. Agnes privately. But, she did stop short of his outstretched arms; giving him a funny look before moving in for a hug.

"It won't take long. I promise."

Sis. Agnes and Brian waited quietly. He begins speaking when he hears the bath water running.

"What's on your mind, Brian?"

Struggling to come up with the words to say, he pauses.

"It's hard to put it in word, Sis. Agnes."

"Perhaps I should sit."

For some reason, this helps.

"I know that we're doing God's work," he begins. "I feel confident that He will protect and help us. But, I can't help worrying that Lyla might get hurt. I hate to say this, but I wish that she would show a little fear sometimes. It's like she think she's wearing a bulletproof vest."

"Perfectly understandable. There's always a little doubt. Some might say it's healthy."

"Really?"

"Absolutely. I have doubts. The challenge is to persevere despite the doubts. In that area, you and Lyla have done a magnificent job, thus far."

"Thank you," he said, clearing his throat. "But, I was wondering. What exactly is our mission?'

Pausing again, he attempts to figure out exactly what it is that concerns him most.

"Will Lyla really become Lyla Washington one day? And will we ever be able to move on with our lives?"

"Well, I can't guarantee the name change. But, in my opinion, she already is Mrs. Washington."

It feels good to Brian to hear this.

"As far as the other matter is concerned, I would say that helping to save the lives of the Pope and Marquis Daniels would be a part of that mission. Exposing Amelia Bradford's killers and the reason behind her murder also seem to be important parts of our mission."

Sis. Agnes wasn't telling him anything that he didn't already know regarding the mission. But, it eased his mind to hear her confirm what Lyla and he already believed.

"Now I have a question for you, Mr. Washington," she continued.

"Sure."

"Would you like a hug - from me?'

"Excuse me?"

"I didn't mean anything by it. I just thought you might be in need of a hug - from me."

He was confused.

"I don't mind hugging you, Sis. Agnes. But, you think that I *need* a hug?"

"Perhaps I'm wrong. But, I usually have a keen sense for these types of things."

He didn't want to be rude. But, he couldn't help laughing at the thought.

"I mean... sure. Why not?"

The funny thing is that to this day he doesn't remember the hug. According to Sis. Agnes, when they hugged he pressed his head against one of her shoulders and fell asleep.

He woke up the next day, feeling rested. Not wanting to jeopardize the elaborate operation on Ansel Road, the three of them checked into another hotel, the new 26-story *Marriot Suites Hotel* on the corner of Clinton and Shaker Heights Boulevard. On the ride over, Sis. Agnes and Brian continued to – as Lyla put it – feel each other out. He sat in the back seat while Lyla drove.

"If you were going to kill the Pope, Sis. Agnes, how would you do it?"

"I would never kill the Pope."

Frustrated by the inability to dream and prophesy at will, Brian thought he might engage Lyla and Sis. Agnes in a little detective work. But speculation, it appeared, wasn't one of her strong suits. He should have dropped the matter, then and there. The question, though, seemed simple and harmless enough. There was a lot on the line, here, including Their safety as well as the Pope's.

"Sis. Agnes, we know that you're not planning to kill the Pope. But I'm not so sure that God is just going to give the answers to all of the questions that we need answered. He hasn't, so far. We're gonna have to figure out some of these things on our own."

"I'm sorry, Brian. I could never even contemplate killing Pope Francis."

"Not even to save his life?"

"I'm sorry."

He looks at Lyla.

"Is she for real? Tell me she's joking."

"I don't have a problem with the two of you engaging in speculation."

"All we've done up to this point is engage in speculation."

There's that Voodoo Queen facial expression again.

"Am I making you uncomfortable, Brian?"

This is starting to sound like the conversation that they had a day earlier.

"That's okay," Sis. Agnes. "You don't have to answer the question. And please don't ask me if I need another hug."

"Maybe it would help. You never know."

He's flabbergasted.

"What are you talking about?"

He looks at Lyla

"Do you have *ANY* clue what she's talking about?"

This was a rhetorical question. Not only did Lyla answer it, however; she came straight out of left field.

"I'll answer the question, Brian; but only if you really want me to."

Taking a moment to reflect on what it is that he missed, he remained flabbergasted. He asked Sis. Agnes a simple question about an impending attempt to take the Pope's life; and somehow he ends up on the rush hour version of the *Oprah Winfrey Show*. Not having the patience to hear a bunch of psychobabble about being uncomfortable around Sis Agnes, he becomes irritated again. But now that Lyla has bought into this nonsense, there's no way to avoid the conversation without it appearing as if he's afraid to hear whatever it is that she has to say.

"You know what, Lyla?" he says, sitting back. "I'd prefer to focus on figuring out how we might save the Pope's life. But, if you and Sis. Agnes are intent on playing Oprah, then – by all means – be my guest."

Not hesitating for a second, Lyla shoots straight from the hip; bringing an annoying grin to Sis. Agnes' face.

"You're afraid of becoming attached to Sis. Agnes because you..."

Brian is speechless; unconvinced — but speechless.

"Are you sure you wouldn't like another hug, Brian?"

He takes a deep, annoyed breath; shaking his head.

"Sis. Agnes, what's this deal with the hugs? If you want a hug, just say so. I'm sure Lyla won't mind... since she thinks I'm afraid of becoming attached to you."

"Leave me out of this," Lyla says, looking back and giggling after stopping at the light.

"Oh now, you want me to leave you out of it. A minute ago you were Oprah Winfrey."

She bursts into laughter.

"It's okay, Brian," Sis. Agnes says, extending the palm of her hand to his face. "I'm going to miss the two of you as well."

He's beyond annoyed and — if the two of them are even half right — completely clueless about his own feelings.

Sis. Agnes' palm finally touches his face.

"Sis. Agnes, please."

The moment that her soft, warm palm is on his forehead, though, his mind goes blank. Seconds later, he closes his eyes and falls fast asleep. He vaguely remembered Lyla helping him walk into the hotel but nothing else. But again, he woke up feeling invigorated. That didn't keep him from having a stern conversation with Sis. Agnes, however. She explained that her little sleeping trick was for his benefit, promising to never do it again.

During the entire time that they spent with Sis. Agnes it was Lyla who insisted that, out of respect for her, an unmarried couple shouldn't engage in sexual intercourse. Needing some sort of release, Brian insisted on sleeping alone while Lyla and Sis. Agnes shared a room. That night, though, Lyla snuck into his room. The next morning he couldn't wait to give her a hard time.

Sis. Agnes was a late sleeper. Lyla and Brian always showered and dressed first. At 7:00 a.m., Lyla had just gotten out of the shower. When she saw his reflection, she ignored him. She looked unusually refreshed and a little guilty.

"Good morning, Lyla," he said with a huge grin.

No response.

"What's wrong? You feeling guilty about something?"

"Shut up!"

"You shut up!"

He stands there until she finishes brushing her teeth. She has an annoyed expression on her face the entire time. For the first time since they met, Lyla is the bad guy. He can't resist rubbing it in.

"I think I'll go tell Sis. Agnes about the prophetic dream that I had last night. It might help with the mission. In the dream I woke up with a strange woman with no panties on straddling my face."

"Come back here."

"I think she was trying to smother me," he laughs. "Instead of looking for a male shooter, maybe we should be looking for a female with her thong pulled to the side."

He bursts into laughter.

"If you don't get back here, you, I'm gonna kill you."

"You know what else I dreamed last night?" he asks, returning to the bathroom.

"Leave me alone," she says, rolling her eyes at him through the mirror.

"You're right. I don't need to wash my face. Let me go say 'good morning' to Sis. Agnes. I think I need another hug."

"Quit playing, Brian."

But Brian keeps walking. Two seconds later, he feels Lyla grabbing him by the hand.

"Why don't you come into the bathroom and wash your face while you tell me about that other dream."

He hesitates a second, savoring the sweet taste of victory and the priceless look on her face. Then he accompanies her to the bathroom, describing a made-up dream as he washes his face.

"Oh man! This dream was awesome! WAFFLES! SAUSAGE! A HAM & CHEESE OMELETTE! AND A NICE, COLD GLASS OF ORANGE JUICE! It was much tastier than this hotel food."

"Where am I gonna get all that, Brian?"

He turns to look at her, face covered in lather.

"Haven't you heard of a grocery store, Wonder Woman?"

"I'm tired, Brian."

"I bet you are."

"What if I did it tomorrow?"

"SIS. AGNES!"

"Okay, boy! I hate you!"

"That's not what you said last night. SIS. AGNES!"

He didn't think that he was speaking loud enough for the snoring Sis. Agnes to hear. His mouth dropped open in surprise when she answered, standing just a few feet outside the bathroom door.

"Did someone call me?"

Speechless now, Brian looks at Lyla; pleading innocence.

"Ooops!"

"I'm cooking breakfast this morning, Sis. Agnes."

"You are?" he smiles. "Thank you! What did Sis. Agnes and I do to earn this special treatment?"

She punches him in the stomach.

"Brian and I are about to go to the grocery store."

"Be careful out there."

"Come over here and give us a hug," he says, still gloating and still a little upset about what happened on the drive to the hotel.

They entered into a three-way hug.

"This is beautiful! Ain't it, Sis. Agnes?"

Sis. Agnes has no clue what's going on but knows that They're up to something. Out of nowhere, he feels a sharp pinch on the back of his arm.

"OUCH!"

"Sorry. I need to cut these nails."

Then, off they went to the grocery store.

Chapter 10

Celeste Returns

On the way back from the grocery store Brian noticed that funny look on Lyla's face again.

"Is everything okay?"

"Yes."

But she keeps staring into the rearview mirror. She puts the right blinker on and slows down as if she's about to merge into the turning lane; but she never merges. She gets back into their original lane. Now, he knows that something is up as she continues to search for something. That's when a dark blue Lexus pulls up beside them. In it are Peter Levin, Father Donovan and two other men. They don't see them, though, as Lyla slows down and makes a quick right turn.

"That was Peter Levin and Father Donovan," he says.

"I know. We saw them on TV yesterday while you were sleeping. Did you know that the Pope was in town today?"

"No I didn't. You think something's gonna happen today, don't you?"

"I'm not sure, but it wouldn't surprise me."

"It wouldn't surprise me, either."

What did surprise Brian was returning to the hotel and finding two unexpected visitors: Pastor Ricky and Celeste.

"How did they know we were here?" he asked Lyla when they were alone in his room.

"I called my brother yesterday while you were sleeping."

"Boy, a whole lot seemed to happen after Sis. Agnes' hugs. Is there anything else that I need to know? Are we sure that Sis. Agnes isn't the killer?"

Lyla just looks at Brian, rolling her eyes.

"How do I know? She did just appear out of nowhere."

"Trust me, Brian. I would know."

"How?"

"Because my gift is like a lie detector."

"Well, how do I know you're not the assassin?"

"Well," she says with a devilish smile, "for one, I'm wearing panties. Why don't you lock the door and help me take them off."

Lyla spent the next thirty minutes convincing him that she wasn't the killer. As she left the room, he was falling asleep with a smile on his face. His next dream was so disturbing, though, that he didn't sleep for long. In it, there was a mass shooting on Public Square as Pope Francis delivered a speech attacking Wall Street. He immediately called his buddy Tim, who made a habit of monitoring the news, to find out when Pope Francis' speech was scheduled.

"It's scheduled two days from now," Tim told Brian, "on Public Square."

When the *Associated Press* reported that evening on the videotape they found on *CURRENT*, however, the entire saga appeared to be over. Bishop Matthias was not only exposed as a fraud; he had become a person of interest in the case involving Marquis Daniel's disappearance and Amelia Bradford's murder. His face was all over the news with reporters asking the same questions:

"Do you know where Marquis Daniels is?"

"Did you kill Amelia Bradford?"

"What do you think of the tape showing Marquis Daniels predicting the rainbow a full week before your prediction?"

Lyla, Sis. Agnes and Brian gave each other high-fives. This whole episode had started with that crazy rainbow prediction. Now that it had been brought to a resolution, he told himself, their role in this caper was over. At first, he didn't bother telling Lyla and Sis. Agnes about the Public Square dream; but it continued to bother him. So that night, when Celeste and Pastor Ricky weren't around, he told them.

"Do you know what direction the shots came from?" Sis. Agnes asked.

"From Tower City.... probably about the fifteenth floor."

Sis. Agnes makes a phone call to someone connected to Pope Francis' inner circle, informing them of an impending plot to kill the Pope. She fills them in on all the details. She hangs up the phone with a look of relief on her face.

"You may have just saved Pope Francis' life."

"I hope so."

Chapter 11

Judgment Day

Finally, the day of Pope Francis' long awaited speech on Poverty in America arrived. But, while they waited for 5:00 PM to arrive, Brian had to deal with another matter.

Under such extraordinary circumstances, he couldn't call Celeste's arrival his worst nightmare; but he dreaded the prospect of being alone with her. She could easily add gasoline to this flammable situation. Based on everything he'd witnessed, they had no reason to trust her. But what bothered him on a deeper level was the fact that any negative consequences that he suffered in connection with her meddling would be a result of his own dishonorable behavior. Saying *"I'm sorry"* didn't seem to be enough to rectify the suffering that he put her through. Even in the midst of this honorable mission, he sensed that God would not let this particular transgression go unchecked.

As he observed her interacting with Lyla as though they were suddenly best friends, he couldn't help thinking that she was up to something. Something just didn't seem right. He had other things to concern myself with for now, though. Needing to talk to Sis. Agnes, he invited her to his room while Lyla entertained Celeste and Pastor Ricky.

"What is it, Brian?" she asked, with a concerned expression on her face.

"I don't want to alarm you, Sis. Agnes. Some of my dreams appear to be inspired by God and some of them are just dreams. It's hard for me to tell the difference."

"Did you have another dream last night?"

"Yes."

"Was it about Pope Francis?"

"Yes. There was shooting again. But this time it was at a new location. In the King-Kennedy Projects."

Brian could tell that she was struggling to make sense of what she had just heard.

"Do you think there's any chance that they changed the location of the speech to the King-Kennedy Projects?"

"I don't know. It's possible. Let me make a phone call."

When the call was over, Sis. Agnes returned and sat down next to him with a ghastly look on her face. He could tell that she feared for Pope Francis' life now more than ever.

"Brian," she says, without getting into details, "I need you and Lyla to accompany me to the speech today."

The new location for the speech had not been announced to the media. Sis. Agnes' contact confirmed that the new, unannounced location was King-Kennedy, indeed.

"So, someone from the pope's inner circle has to be in on the assassination plot."

"I'm afraid so."

Sis. Agnes looks as though she can use a hug now.

"We might be his only hope."

"Don't worry, Sis. Agnes. We have God on our side."

"Do you know how we nuns define the word responsibility?"

"No, how do you define it?"

"Our RESPONSE to God's ABILITY. God has given you and Lyla the ability to save Pope Francis. You have to go with me today."

"Sure Sis. Agnes. Pope Francis is a good man. He washed the feet of female prison inmates. He's the only pope that I can think of that has conducted himself in the spirit of Jesus Christ."

When Sis. Agnes and Brian went next door to fill Lyla in on the dream and their new plan, Brian was happy to discover that Pastor Ricky and Celeste had checked into their own room on a different floor.

After lunch, Lyla and Sis. Agnes played dominoes while he stretched, knocked-out five sets of push-ups and showered. He hadn't even finished dressing when two cars, filled with agents from the *Department of Homeland Security,* pulled into the hotel parking lot.

Looking out of the 24th floor hotel room window Sis. Agnes calmly announced, "They're here."

Making her way to a duffle bag, she produces three wrinkled jackets.

"Here," she said, "put these on."

He couldn't help wondering how putting jackets on would help.

"Are these bulletproof?"

"No."

"Then why do we need them?"

"No time to explain. Just make sure you buckle all three belts tightly, especially beneath the armpits."

This didn't sound right. But Sis. Agnes was right about one thing: time was precious.

"Where are they?"

"I don't know," he responds, confused.

Lyla points to her ear.

"Blue-tooth."

Shaking her head now, "When this is over we need to get you a pair of glasses."

"They're in the lobby.... At the front desk."

"Uh, shouldn't we be leaving?"

"Not yet. We don't want to hit the ground until our ride is here."

Brian looks at Lyla.

"Hit the ground?"

But, Lyla - Ms. Wonder Woman - doesn't see a problem with the plan.

"You didn't hear her stutter," she says, before realizing that he's afraid for both their lives.

"Haven't you ever been skydiving?"

"Hell no! Black people don't skydive!"

"Brian, I promise you," she says, grabbing his hand gently, "you can do this."

"Boy," he says, looking at her, "I gotta get me some of this faith. You're telling me that these flimsy looking jackets are parachutes and that you expect us to jump out of a 24th floor window?"

"Don't worry. I've practiced with them plenty of times."

"That's a relief."

'Time to go!" Sis. Agnes shouts, running towards the door. "Grab the cord *before* you jump and pull it as soon as you feel yourself dropping."

In the hallway, they see that the elevator is at the sixteenth floor.

"Wait!" Lyla shouts to Sis. Agnes.

"I'm sorry. There's no time."

But Lyla grabs her by the arm.

"You have to go first; then I'll go. That way Brian won't feel like we're jumping to our deaths. Otherwise, we won't do it."

Sis. Agnes studies his face for a split second. Then she sees that the elevator is at the twentieth floor.

"Okay. But we have to go – *NOW!*"

With this, she and Lyla take off down the hall towards a slightly opened window. Brian watches the elevator hit the twenty-first floor then the twenty second. When it hits the twenty-third floor he looks down the hallway and sees that Sis. Agnes has already jumped.

"*FUCK!*"

"*COME ON, BRIAN!*" Lyla shouts.

His adrenalin kicks into overdrive when he sees the light for the twenty-fourth floor light up.

"*IT OPENED!*" Lyla yelled, still trying to assure him that everything would okay.

"*OKAY!*" he yells back, running down the hallway now. "*GO!*"

Seeing the men get off the elevator, running behind him, Lyla refuses to jump without Brian. He needs to buy some time. So, he takes off a tennis shoe and flings it as hard as he can at the leader of the pack, slowing him down enough that a couple of the other men crash into him from behind.

"HURRY UP, LYLA!" he yells. "I'M COMING!"

But, she continues to wait. When he reaches her, she yells: *"LET'S JUMP TOGETHER!"*

With that, they hold hands and jump.

To this day, he's not sure what would have happened had Lyla not waited on him. He remembers Sis. Agnes mentioning a cord. But, in the middle of all the commotion, this critical piece of information somehow escaped his attention.

"OH, MY GOD!" he yells, free-falling from the twenty-fourth floor. Mentally frozen, he had just about come to grips with the fact that Lyla and he had spent their last days on the planet when she reached out and pulled his cord. When the parachute opened, decreasing the speed of his drop so much that he was actually able to think again, all he could do was thank the Lord and Savior for saving him from certain death. He didn't actually see Lyla pull the cord of her own parachute. But seconds later, the two of them were face to face; almost close enough to touch hands. Descending more slowly now, he looked at Lyla, wondering what he had done to deserve such a beautiful, special woman.

"Hurry up!" Sis. Agnes yells when they hit the ground.

Helping them out of the parachute jackets first, she then directs them to the car that is waiting for them. Scared and relieved, adrenaline rushes through his body.

"Lyla, what on earth is wrong with you?" he yells at her. "Some crazy lady from another planet straps a belt around your chest and you jump out of a 20-story window?"

"We're safe," she smiles.

"I know. Thank God. I love you, girl. You can't keep scaring me like this."

She grabs his face and kisses him.

"The next time some crazy lady from another planet saves your life make sure you say 'thank you.' Right, Sis. Agnes?"

"Thank you, Sis. Agnes," Lyla repeats, louder this time.

"You're welcome, but we still have important business to take care of before we celebrate."

"Anybody ever told you that you look like Emeli Sande?" Brian finally asks her.

"Who's Emeli Sande?"

"A singer, a pretty hot one."

"Are you trying to tell me that you think I'm hot, Brian Washington?'

"No. I mean, you are pretty hot for a nun. But, more importantly, you just saved our lives. In case I haven't said it before, thank you."

"You're welcome."

"Where are we headed?" the driver of the car asks.

Sis. Agnes looks at Brian. After surveying their location, he instructs the driver to make a right before turning left on Larchmere.

They arrived at 6001 Woodland Avenue at shortly after noon.

What he hadn't counted on was Pastor Ricky and Celeste accompanying them to King-Kennedy. In the dream, the shots were fired from the Carl Stokes building; the only tall building close to the *King-Kennedy Projects*. So, they posted up in the lobby there, hoping that Lyla could get a read on the shooter as soon as he entered the building. Of course, there was the possibility that he might already be in the building.

Brian didn't like the way that Celeste kept staring at him. He had avoided her as much as he could. When she walked over and invited him to meet her outside for a private discussion, he wanted to refuse. But, how could he? It was time to face the music.

"I need to talk to you about something," she says, "and I doubt that you would want Lyla and Ricky to hear what I have to say."

The butterflies in his stomach seemed to catch fire as she said these words. 'Oh my goodness,' he thought, feeling a little dizzy. 'It's best to get it over with now. If Celeste knows about my involvement with her arrest, it's only a matter of time before Lyla and the rest of the family finds out. God sure doesn't make things easy.' The timing couldn't have been any worst. 'No matter what happens to me personally, I still have to do everything in my power to save Pope Francis.' Maybe he was showing signs of growth. But the blessings, it seemed, would have to come on another day.

He waited until Lyla made another round of the floors with Sis. Agnes before signaling Celeste that he was ready to talk. This turned out to be a huge mistake.

Standing out in the mall area of the Carl Stokes Building, Celeste is livid. He doesn't remember everything she said, but he did remember these words:

"I sat in jail for months because of you. From now on, you can just call me Karma. And believe me when I tell you this, Karma is a mothafucka."

After a while it occurs to him that Celeste's loud talking isn't rooted in her emotions. At first, he assumes that she wants Lyla to hear her. But, why go through all this when she could just tell Lyla what happened? The moment that he sees Father Donovan's face, he realizes that it's a set-up. He would learn later that Celeste had run into Father Donovan in their rooms after they jumped out of the window.

She didn't know that he planned to kill all the jumpers, but she was more than happy to accept $1,000 in exchange for leading him to Brian. He could tell that Celeste was horrified when she saw Father Donovan marching towards Brian, pistol pointed directly at his chest.

Brian never thought he'd survive the first gunshot wound. As he stood in shock, Father Donovan walked towards him deliberately; aiming carefully. Brian heard shots ring out in the distance as three more bullets pierced his chest. Falling to the ground, his thoughts drifted automatically to his family and Lyla. Lying suddenly in a puddle of blood, he cherished every moment with them; acknowledging Lyla as a personal, if temporary, blessing from God.

By the time he regained consciousness, the mission was over. Lyla identified one of the shooters; a friend of Sis. Agnes intercepted a round of bullets from a second. Hit three times, however, Pope Francis still lied in a hospital bed.

As far as Brian's own injuries, he still feels grateful today that the lasting impact on his health was minimal. None of the bullets hit within two inches of the heart muscle. The scars serve as a reminder of the folly of vengeance and of taking spiritual matters into one's own hands.

"Vengeance is mine; I will repay, saith the Lord."
(Roman 12:19)

"Don't let evil conquer you, but conquer evil by doing good."

(Romans 12:21)

"Even when you are chased by those that seek to kill you, your life is safe in the care of the Lord your God, secure in His treasure pouch!"

(1 Samuel 25:29)

These are scriptures that Brian will never forget.

Finally, he will always remember those life-shaking, life-shaping words of Ephesians 6:12:

> "For we are not fighting against flesh-and-blood enemies, but against evil rulers and authorities of the unseen world, against mighty powers in this dark word, and against evil spirits in the Heavenly places."

In these words, he found the power to forgive; clearing the pathway to complete transformation and to a loving, God-centered relationship with one of God's special people.

Celeste was a no-show at the next Johnson family gathering. That didn't surprise Brian. But he was surprised to receive a phone call from her toward the end of the gathering. She had expected him to make her involvement in his shooting the major topic of conversation. Word got back to her that no one even raised the subject. Brian never told on her. They had a good conversation. Over the ensuing weeks, it was a pleasure to watch her transform into a genuinely beautiful person. Sometimes he wondered where things had ever gone wrong. But, watching her and Lyla laugh and talk the way loving cousins are supposed to, it no longer seemed to matter. Lyla was happy. All glory to God. That is why we praise and worship Him.

Regarding the mission, Lyla and Brian were unclear about what they had accomplished.

Marquis Daniels was finally in safe hands. Bishop Matthias and Peter Levin were exposed and under congressional investigation. The immediate crisis appeared to be over. Yet, with Pope Francis confined to Cleveland Clinic's Intensive Care Unit, trouble seemed to loom on the horizon. Pope Francis had survived the shooting. But Cardinal Bernadine, the epicenter of this nefarious plot, was still poised to become the next pope.

"You two have accomplished more than you realize," Sis. Agnes says, sensing their disappointment. "You helped enlighten the people and probably saved the Pope's life."

Even if this was true, the extraordinary expectations that came with such amazing spiritual gifts made the outcome feel anti-climatic. After a dedicated effort and so many risks, Pope Francis still ended up getting shot. This is what, for lack of a better word, *surprised* them the most. They'd get over it, eventually. But Sis. Agnes, approaching with an unusual stare, lifts their spirits for a lifetime.

Jeff Mixon

As Sis. Agnes's palms slowly approaches their faces, Lyla and Brian become captivated by a strange, peaceful aura. Eyes fastened shut now; they see a most amazing vision of the sun. This is followed by thick, white clouds - blowing gently in a tropical breeze. The dull whistling of the wind grows louder. Lyla and Brian find each other's hands; aware somehow of the gravity of what they're about to see. Sis. Agnes is no longer present. She appears in the vision, singing in an empty night club. The song, *My Kind of Love*, is familiar. The meaning of the song feels different, though. She's singing to the mortal, suffering Jesus. The walls of the club collapse without warning. They see the wind-blown clouds. The sun rises slowly beneath the approaching clouds. There He is! Standing atop the clouds in His glorious majesty is the Lord and Savior, Christ Jesus!

Epilogue

To our peril, we ignore the principles and events and communications of the *Heavenly Places*. We ignore the well-known fact that humans are born with different personality traits, different spiritual gifts and different callings. Stubbornly, we use the same parenting approach in tending to the natural artist that we use to raise the natural administrator. We raise those endowed with noble natures – *the chosen* – the same as those endowed with more simple natures. In ignoring God's plan for our salvation, we usually make a mess of things. But God is all-knowing, all-loving and forever faithful. Consequently, even the messes that we make will inevitably lead to revelations designed to free us from bondage to pride, self-idolatry and self-deception.

Lyla and her brother, Pastor Ricky, were unusual in the way they maintained a partnership with the positive forces of the *Heavenly Places*. Lyla and Ricky didn't just read the Bible, they lived it.

From a *Heavenly* perspective, Celeste also played a critical role. Her behavior strengthened Lyla's reliance on God. In activating Brian's vengeful nature, Celeste sets off a sequence of spiritual events with perfect timing.

Brian didn't have an open relationship with God before meeting Lyla. But his propensity for vengeance was always directed against those who would harm God's people. He couldn't explain how or why he was endowed with the spiritual gift of prophetic dreams for a short, critical time period. His guess is that Lyla's unconditional love unblocked the channel to a partnership with God. After establishing a right relationship with God through surrender, he entered into this partnership gratefully. People must recognize God's rightful place as the center of our lives and as the center of all things. These human partnerships are only necessary because of God's unwavering respect for the most precious bestowed up man – the gift of free will. It is an essential part of the process of transforming human beings into god-like entities.

People ignore their Creator at their own peril.

For only the mutual love between people can save them from the unspeakable evil and deception of a world that cherishes illusions over God's truth and love.

Brian reminds himself each day of Prophet Ellen G. White's warning:

"Whatever we cherish that tends to lessen our love for God or to interfere with the service due Him, of that do we make a god."

Even in hearing these words, most people fail to grasp their existential implications. Fortunately, many others will. Jesus' true followers can't help but recognize the voice of cosmic truth and reason.

In the year 2021, the necessary ingredients converged in the lives of ordinary men and women as it had been planned long ago. They heard God's call, responding in faith and obedience with temporary spiritual gifts. There were brief moments of doubt and concern for each other's safety; but those moments never prevailed. There were days when Brian thought that Lyla was taking on too many risks and responsibilities. But deep inside, they knew that God would protect them. If He didn't, as in the case of Pastor Ricky, who later was assassinated by rogue operatives within the *Department of Homeland Security*, it was only because He had an even greater assignment awaiting in the *Eternal World*.

Is the year 2021 meant to be prophetic? Of course not! For the scriptures say at Matthew 24: 36:

Jeff Mixon

"Concerning that day and the hour nobody knows, neither the angels of the heavens nor the Son, but only the Father."

Time is a concept that cannot be judged in human terms for as brought out at 2Peter 3: 8, 9, which informs:

"... one day is with God as a thousand years and a thousand years as one day. God is not slow respecting His promise, as some people consider slowness, but He is patient with you because He does not desire any to be destroyed but desires all to attain to repentance."

The details of how things will eventually play out remains a mystery. The success in accomplishing the specific task before us, however, is never really in doubt when we abide unceasingly by the will of our *powerful, faithful Companion*.

For as Matthew 22:14 tells us:

Many are called, but we were *chosen*.

About The Author

"**T**hough unworthy, God has graciously allowed me to enter into a partnership with him; because I understand that my worth depends wholly upon obedience to His will. Haunted, like most, by glaring character flaws; a friend reminded me often: '*God doesn't pick the qualified. He qualifies the picked*.' With no further excuse to avoid the rocky path that God has chosen for me, I began writing this book and engaging in local politics in a manner that I knew might engender a backlash. Serving God seldom occurs without trials and tribulations."

A writer, children's advocate, educator, talk radio show host and grassroots politician, Jeff Mixon believes that his specific purpose in life is outlined in the *Book of Malachi*, chapter 4:5-6. A broader purpose, he reveals, is to understand the world in a way that allows him to remain loyal to God's purpose – even when the going gets tough. Believing that *knowledge* is virtue and that true wisdom comes from God, Jeff skillfully influenced the movement to "separate the wheat from the chaff" within the *Cuyahoga County Democratic Party*.

Paraphrasing Socrates in an op-ed piece lambasting the *Cuyahoga County Democratic Party* and corporate-dominated *non-competitive* political districts, he writes: "You have forgotten again, my friends, that the law is not concerned to make any one class especially happy, but to ensure the welfare of the commonwealth as a whole." Jeff is currently a member of the *Cuyahoga County Democratic Party's* Executive Committee.

The second child, of seven, to attend college, Jeff Mixon holds a bachelors degree in psychology from Case Western Reserve University and a master's degree in education from Kent State University.

Save

Our

SOULS

Volume 2

Jeff Mixon

www.ingramcontent.com/pod-product-compliance
Lightning Source LLC
Chambersburg PA
CBHW060114260626
47160CB00005B/1891